NYX'S BLADE

THE KHIMMER CHRONICLES

KEVIN A DAVIS

For April
She has supported me throughout the grueling process of
bringing the Khimmer Chronicles to life.

In Memory of David Farland.
A guiding teacher who was always passionate about
mentorship and writing. You are loved and missed.

CONTENTS

NYX'S BLADE

This is the story of how Ahnjii becomes stranded on Earth. The narrative encompasses two worlds and how she comes to meet the fae on Earth.

For those of you who are reading this before the series, I've included the first chapter to *Wight's Wrath: Book One of the Khimmer Chronicles*.

If you've already started or finished the Khimmer Chronicles, then this novella will help fill in some of Ahnjii's history.

CHAPTER 1

I spun so fast that I bumped my face into the car window. "Stop! What is that?"

Tyler slowed, but continued to drive away from the strange person. "I can't stop here, Ahnjii." They gestured to the road and other cars. "Besides, I'm already late for the call."

"It had big ears, like the other one I saw." I swung around to look at the man dwindling in the distance. He was walking in the opposite direction along the grass beside the road. I could only make out dirty blond hair, but I'd seen the ears. "Like a —"

What do they call it? I thought to Khimmer, the mind of my Nightarmor. I sent the image.

Horse, Mistress.

"He had horse's ears poking up to the top of his head." I mimicked by placing both hands to my temples and pointing up.

Tyler glanced over and smiled. They'd shadowed underneath their eyes today. "Cute. Cosplay, perhaps?"

Khimmer, translate?

A form of masquerade, Mistress.

Had it been? It looked so real. I'd seen it before on a different person. There'd also been the driver with a dog's muzzle who had driven past us on a road, but Tyler had thought maybe I'd seen a mask. It couldn't have been human like us. There were strange people on Earth.

"I don't know." I settled back into my seat, adjusting the harness.

I wanted to convince Tyler to turn around, but they had some new internet cause. Deanna, their sister, complained it would get them in trouble again. Supposedly, a similar issue had caused Tyler to be in Slovenia, hunted by thugs, when I'd arrived on Earth. We never would have met otherwise. Tyler called it fate.

I *had* seen something new and strange on Earth. *How far is this road from the house, if I were to walk?* I thought to Khimmer.

Half an hour, Mistress.

Tomorrow, I would have Khimmer lead me back about the same time. Perhaps this tall-eared person returned home from work on a schedule. Routines were very common; I'd relied on them for my assassinations on Duruce.

We pulled onto the street where Tyler and Deanna's family owned a mansion. They seemed quite rich, though I'd never met the parents.

"I'm going to be busy this evening." Tyler tapped the steering wheel with one finger in a quick tempo. "Deanna and John plan on eating at the sports bar tonight. You could hang with them."

I considered going with Deanna and John, but I preferred hanging with Tyler. "I might just read." I'd picked through many of Tyler's books, and they had helped me understand their language.

"Always a good idea." Tyler stopped tapping.

We turned the corner and parked. The family estate covered a corner lot with large trees, flowering bushes, and thin strips of grass. In their neighborhood there were other houses as impressive to me, but Deanna claimed her family weren't rich or nobles. She didn't lie when she said it, but I believed differently. Tallahassee had many sections with tiny houses, broken ones, or buildings where many people lived in apartments.

Children called to each other from the neighboring building. Tyler and Deanna had two buildings. One large warehouse structure had a basketball court inside that we used as a roller skating rink. I'd grown quite good at the activity. Perhaps I would skate alone tonight.

I couldn't help wondering about the man with tall ears. That interested me more than a book or watching sports with Deanna and John at some tavern. I unharnessed myself from the seat of the vehicle Tyler called a Prius. I still had no idea how it moved, but they promised me it wasn't magic.

Tomorrow I would look for this strange person. I stepped out my door. "Maybe I'll skate." The humid air smelled like exhaust with hints of nearby flowers.

"Good call, then read afterward." Tyler led the way to the house. They wore all black clothes: a long-sleeved tight top, baggy knee-length trousers, and black boots.

When I followed them in, the house smelled like old, wilted flowers from the electric incense Deanna plugged into all the walls. Her cats thumped down the stairs ahead of her.

"Tyler, you still got your thing tonight? Ahnjii, you're with us then. John will be home on time, and we'll go over to the bar. We'll practice your English." Deanna had the same black hair as her sibling, Tyler. As did I, but she had hers tied back into a ponytail. Except for their flared nostrils at the ends of their straight noses, we could have been cousins.

"I was going to skate and read," I said.

"Nonsense. Tyler will get into a foul mood over this whole inflated crisis. Come hang with me and John." She picked up one of her orange tabbies and confronted me as she stroked its neck. "Socialize. You hang out with Tyler too much, and they'll make you believe there's nothing but injustice and horror. You're not like that. You've got a healthy optimism. Don't lose it."

I sighed. I didn't want to disappoint her.

In the end, I did enjoy spending the night with Deanna at least. John had never accepted me and just ignored me as usual. Deanna kept me from picking up one of the local college students for sex, but I had fun anyway. When we got home, Tyler barely spoke two sentences before returning to their computer.

"Night," I said when I left Tyler's doorway. Deanna had housed me in the spare room.

"Good night." Tyler's tone spoke of their distraction. I could hear their typing as I drifted off to sleep. They didn't get up until lunchtime the next day.

"How'd your thing go?" I asked.

Tyler's expression soured at my question. They were making coffee with the carafe and plunger. "Idiots. Everyone wants to get distracted about the politics, but these people need solutions, water, now." They shook their head and waved off the comment. "Did you have a good night?"

I nodded. The aroma of Tyler's coffee had me wanting more tea. "I'm going to walk up to that road, the one where I saw the big-eared guy."

"Miccosukee Road? Want company?" Tyler hadn't put on any make-up yet, and their eyes were bloodshot. They were attractive no matter how they looked.

"I'd love it, but I want to get there at the same time as yesterday, so we've got a couple hours. Wanna skate?"

"We'll drive." Tyler nodded, pointing to their coffee mug. "After."

If we hadn't become such good friends, the only true friend I'd ever had, I would have considered sex with them. I just couldn't overcome my Aegis monk traditions enough to even entertain the thought for more than a second. Coffee with Tyler turned into a quick veggie burger and a long explanation of aquifers, which I tried to understand. We got in a short skate, though I couldn't relax, and my mouth went dry too quickly. My thoughts would roam, eventually circling around the strange ears.

After lunch, skating, and a quick shower, I finally paraded behind Tyler out to their car. My heart raced at the idea of finding this person. I flicked the ends of my braid nervously. Tyler seemed sure that it had been some masquerade of sorts, and if we found the man, he wouldn't still have the ears on. The images they'd shown me on my phone weren't the same as the tall ears poking up through the blond hair.

"Normally, I'm the obsessed one," Tyler said with a grin. "Good to see you get excited about this."

I punched them in the shoulder like the people did at the bar. "You're teasing me."

Tyler frowned. "Yeah."

Had I insulted them? I still had a hard time with Earth traditions compared to my world. Duruce had customs that varied with each culture, but I had monks to help in studying those.

Did I do it wrong?

The action seemed appropriate last night, Mistress.

"This is Miccosukee Road," Tyler said as they turned the corner.

I leaned forward with my pulse rising. I recognized buildings as we drove by, but focused on the sidewalks. We hadn't gone a minute before I spotted the man. "There, up there." The harness pinned me back.

"Got it." Tyler moved to the side closest to the person and slowed.

The man had blond hair and a slow stride. His ears had tufts of hair that tipped over the top of his head.

We passed him slowly with a car beeping before they went around us. "No cosplay," Tyler said.

I twisted in my seat. "Pull over. What is he then?"

"Just some guy." Tyler pointed to a street ahead. "I'll pull in there. Are you sure you should bother him?"

"Look at the ears."

"Normal ears." Tyler's voice sounded suspicious.

How could they not see them? "Those aren't normal," I insisted. Surely they'd notice when we got out.

Tyler pulled to the side of a brick building at the corner, and I already had my harness unclasped. Excitedly I ran out to the road ahead of them.

The blond-haired man had almost reached me when I stepped onto the sidewalk. Cars whizzed past, and the fumes hung heavy in the heat.

"Hi, I'm Ahnjii. What are you?" I pointed to my own ears. "I saw you yesterday . . ."

The man's already pale skin blanched, and he stopped three paces from me. His tall ears twitched. He had fingers that were just longer than a human's.

I'd said something wrong. His expression turned terrified, and his light-colored eyes flicked toward Tyler walking up to us. The person looked trapped.

"I'm sorry," I said. "I haven't met any non-humans before, and I saw you walking yesterday."

The man lifted a hand and touched his ear as if they'd been hidden until I exposed them. I hadn't done anything. The blond-haired man bolted away as if his life depended on it.

"Charming, aren't you?" Tyler laughed.

I turned as they stepped by my side. "You saw the ears, didn't you?"

Tyler rested their hand on my shoulder. "He had normal ears, Ahnjii."

Cars sped by us spewing fumes. The strange Earth sun sat high in the sky. The odd person turned off the sidewalk and disappeared from my sight. I didn't belong on this world. My duty belonged elsewhere.

I took a deep breath. Tyler couldn't see the ears. I could. It was all a waste of time.

How?

I don't know, Mistress. Could it be related to your truthsense?

I sucked in my breath and remembered the woman, the aunt of the kid I helped, who had told me I would end up on Earth. I hadn't understood her words. "Where you go, you will find others that hide behind a lie, but they will not be able to hide from you."

At the time, I'd dismissed the prophecy. Now, I had to be concerned about everything she'd told me. I needed to get home to Duruce.

"When do you think Deanna will let us go back and search for my way home?" I asked Tyler, but they didn't answer. We'd had this conversation too often.

CHAPTER 2

Cɪᴛʏ ᴏꜰ Tᴏsᴇ, nation of Dallobese - Duruce

I clung to the outside of Kloro's mansion with tiny spikes that protruded from Nightarmor's boots and gauntlets. For the past hour, I had dug them into the dry mortar between shaded stones. The merchant's privy extended out three feet, allowing me a crevice shaded from the sun and hidden from prying eyes. Three stories down, the cesspit leaked fumes. The sickly-sweet stench of sewage wafted in the air. Birds called from the surrounding trees, but the grounds below me were empty and quiet. The morning bell had yet to ring. Kloro would be waking soon to use his privy. The merchant baron's internal clock had been consistent over the past week.

Kloro's ancestors had been foolish enough to provide ventilation in the form of narrow slits between blocks. I doubted it diffused the smell inside the privy, but it gave me enough space for Nightarmor's sword to slide in.

Queen Meihlia desired him dead, and he'd facilitated

my mission with a routine and opportunity. She hadn't required that anyone know I'd killed him as her First Assassin, so I planned a quieter option. It made for an easier escape.

In a different city in Dallobese, I'd been required to provide a public assassination last month. The escape had required me disabling a guard and leaving him alive but injured and likely out of a vocation. I didn't like that.

A gate slapped closed on the grounds of a neighboring mansion, and I cautioned a quick glance. I had requested a light armor, but that still included a thin helmet without eye slits, so my vision was through Khimmer. People and animals would show as orange and yellow. My pulse rose, though nothing moved within our sight. Few people in the merchant city of Tose woke before the morning bell, except servants.

I turned back to my focus. Through the stone, the dim figure of Kloro still slept as a horizontal orange shape.

No servants had come to his room. Yesterday, he hadn't rung their bell until after his excursion to the privy. They'd been prompt, so I hoped this was his routine; otherwise, I'd risk an alarm. In another situation, I would have confirmed the daily regimen, but hanging on the side of the mansion I could be spotted, even through the many trees.

I let out a quiet breath and checked the angle of my sword. My arm muscles needed constant flexing, or I'd be stiff. What I didn't want was for the sword to scrape on stone.

I drew a deep breath as Kloro stirred. The movement showed as no more than fluctuation in Khimmer's vision between shades of yellow and orange.

His arm lifted as if to wipe his face. A moment later, his

torso rose. Kloro let out a grumbling yawn, and wood creaked as he slid his feet off the bed.

I relaxed to even breathing and focused where I imagined his head would be in the privy. My target would be his neck. A soft, quick push and a twist would finish the job.

A glass clinked against a pitcher, and Kloro tilted his head back to drink. Why would he need a beverage before taking a piss?

Slowly, Kloro made his way toward me. The man waddled.

The door to the privy creaked open, and I kept my breathing steady despite a racing pulse. His clothing rustled.

He paused, turned, and surprisingly started to sit. I'd nearly jabbed when the back of his skull dropped below my strike zone.

What man sat to piss? His head descended below the ventilation slit. I would have to angle high to reach his neck. The gap between the stones might be too tight and bind the sword when I pushed.

Teeth clenched, I lifted my right elbow. Khimmer's vision highlighted the man's features in detail, even through the wall. I could have waited, retreated and returned, or looked for a different opportunity. Instead, my muscles already tense, I took my shot. Nightarmor's metal sword tip scraped against stone.

For a wide man, Kloro jumped quickly.

The tip of Nightarmor's sword plunged under his jaw near his ear. The impact pushed Kloro away from me and tilted his body. As I skewered his head, my sword guard shoved against the rough stone.

He died instantly, and his body weighed on my sword. *The Queen's Will be done.*

Partial retract, I thought to Khimmer.

They had already reacted. Liquid metal rolled down the blade and was absorbed. *Yes, Mistress.*

I withdrew the remainder, had it reshaped into a more functional, double-edged short sword, and placed it against my back where Nightarmor held it.

Using the spikes on boots and thumbs, I began my descent. The stench worsened as I climbed down.

The birds had not stopped calling to each other. However, no one called out a warning from gardens or mansion. I focused on the dry mortar cracks between the stones.

Khimmer, anyone? They could alert me if someone spotted my escape. That knowledge had saved my life before.

No one, Mistress.

Once I left Kloro's grounds, I would have three days travel back to Vale Aganor and my Queen. A full day would be getting out of Dallobese. My order, the Aegis monks, had an agent waiting for me near the border. I would have to contact them before crossing, then finalize my escape. Conditions and options changed quickly along the trade routes that connected Dallobese and Vale Aganor. Our countries shared a common border, but I would need a clear path without questions. If any suspected my identity, I would have to fight my way through the rest of the country.

I had nearly failed in the assassination. The mission would have been completed, but with Kloro warned, it would have taken me much longer.

My mentor, Turben, would say I acted rashly in striking when the situation changed beyond my expectation, but it had worked. He always accused me of not putting the time or thought into my kills. He'd warned that my reliance on Nightarmor would be my downfall. *Not today.*

I leaped the last few feet, and Khimmer adjusted Nightarmor to absorb the impact. Leaves and gravel crunched as I spun.

The grounds stretched from my right to a thick stand of trees in the back. I faced the gardens and paths between the mansion and the stone wall that bordered the neighbor's lands.

There were no cries from above, and Kloro's grounds were clear.

Remove armor, I thought to Khimmer.

Yes, Mistress.

Nightarmor melted off me, leaving both fresh and foul air to assault my sweating face. It formed bangles and bracelets on my forearms, a thin choker which circled my throat, and armbands under the blue artisan's smock I wore. Winding around my waist, it made a dull black belt. Tall boots of flexible metal thickened around my feet and calves.

I flipped my black braid forward and stroked the tip as I walked. My path crossed gardens and stone as I angled for the bordering stone wall. Intending to keep with my original escape plan, I wondered about the swinging gate from earlier.

At the front of my target's property were stables and a gardener's shed blocking my view of his drive or the street beyond. It would not be good to risk alerting the horses or the stable hands who slept there.

The tall spires of a Rhys temple rose farther inside the city. Birds trailed in a flock around the gray points.

I was only a few steps from the stone wall which rose a head higher than me.

Khimmer?

One worker at the back of the property, Mistress. They are turned away from you.

Taking the wall after three quick strides, I vaulted to the top, avoided the leaves and mulch of a garden, and dropped quietly to the grass of the neighboring mansion.

I jogged toward the gate at the front of the property, probably the same that I'd heard earlier. My pulse had slowed with the climb, and my heart beat steadily with the exertion.

Turben would dismiss my escape as luck and chastise my kill, but he always did. A sparring session would be ordered, and I'd walk away bruised. The Aegis monks were not family, but they had raised me and taught me strength and duty. I would have preferred to be friends, but we were not allowed that risk. As an assassin, anyone close to me could be used against me, and all of Duruce knew that I was the Queen's First Assassin.

Flowering red bushes scented the walk, and a fat tan bird hopped away lazily at my approach. As I passed through the gate, I noted two servants running along cobblestones of the street ahead of me. They carried no packages, so I assumed they had been sent off with early morning messages. Their focus never shifted toward me.

The temple of Rhys dominated the opposite side of the wide road. The priests and priestesses were tending their gardens, as they did at all hours. Dressed in little more than loose pants and aprons, they were an attractive group, but I had no time for idle thoughts.

The shops that bordered each side were still quiet. The wind had shifted to scents of horses and manure.

The city would wake as I escaped. Craftsmen and shopkeepers would open and ring noise into the streets while carts would clatter down cobblestones.

The servants of Kloro would eventually check on him, after he did not ring for them in a reasonable amount of time. I could not know how long they would consider appropriate, but I doubted anyone would remember a young artisan walking the streets before the morning bells.

I'd completed my task and had an exit plan. My satchel and water bag were already hidden nearby, close to the fairgrounds. Making my way to my hiding place, I kept an eye on the early morning traffic which slowly emerged from the city's buildings.

The Silari wagoners were always loose with their tongues when they drank past the evening bells. Thanks to Khimmer, I knew their language. Experience told me the coin it would take to join their morning caravan.

I strolled toward the Silari as they harnessed horses. A wide man and a tall woman laughed as they cinched belts while a younger boy struggled to position a reluctant horse at the front of a green-painted wagon.

"Don't be afraid of him, Lensu," the woman called out in their sing-song language.

The Silari wore colorful vests with their loose pants, though these had long knives strapped at their waists. Their camp, on the trampled grass of the fairgrounds, had been broken down and the three wagons nearly readied for travel. The scent of horse dung and quenched fires drifted in the air.

Match their blade on my belt.

Yes, Mistress.

Nightarmor shifted at my left hip, but I never lost a stride.

"Good morrow. Where are you headed?" I asked the woman in her language.

She had short dark hair and paused to face me with a frown. "Why do you care?"

I ignored her tone and laughed. "I have no cares at the moment. My master let me go, and I'm off to a new city or town that has less stench."

Her expression softened as I spoke, and the edges of her mouth nearly lifted by the end. "Alone? That is a risk on these roads."

I smiled wider and tapped the blade at my hip. "This is not my first town."

Her companion studied me with a suspicious face, but the woman had started to warm to me. "How old are you?"

"Twenty-nine," I lied. The extra three years would give her more confidence in my maturity.

She glanced at her companion and sighed. "We cannot have passengers."

My truthsense triggered, and I knew she lied. "I have coin to save my boots, if you're headed toward Vale Aganor." Digging into the pouch in Nightarmor's simple belt, I produced two silvers. "I'm fair with a blade if there's trouble." Dallobese had more raiders than Vale Aganor and Tahnet combined.

She glanced at a bear of a man with a thick beard and red vest who tethered horses at the first wagon. "I can ask."

I placed the coins in her hand. "Thank you."

As she strolled toward the red-vested man, I turned to her companion. He continued to work the straps and gear of his horse. The young boy had lost ground with his defiant charge.

I gestured with a smile. "Mind if I help? Dad had a mare that hated her stall, but I always managed."

He snorted, wiped his hand down his blue and green vest, and jerked his head toward the boy. "Suit yourself."

His voice low and rumbling, he managed a gruff tone with ease.

I bounced to action and had my hands busy when the woman reached the red-vested leader and they both looked over. I'd lied about a dad and had less understanding of horses than the boy, but I appeared engaged.

By the time she returned, the boy had managed to clasp the collar which the horse wore to the cart, and we seemed successful. There were more buckles and links he worked, but I stepped back to meet her.

The coins were gone from her hand. "Name's Sinda." She nodded her head toward the large man. "Ginshai. The boy's new, Lensu. You're with us. My problem, he says."

The woman spoke the truth with each statement. If they didn't hide their names, they likely would be reputable merchants.

Relieved and excited, I bounced. "Thank you. I'm Ahnette." I hadn't used the name in a while, and it spoke of Dallobese roots.

The morning bells rang across the city. Had they found my target yet?

Sinda smiled and gestured toward the wagon. "Stow your gear; we're ready to go."

I tossed my bag inside, left the water bag on my shoulder, and vaulted over the rail. The bed of the wagon had been stacked with musty sacks of beans and grain. The Silari caravans acted as general merchants from their country through Dallobese because much of their homeland was too mountainous and separated by water to do much more than mine ore, smelter, and smith.

Sinda smacked a grumbling Ginshai as they climbed to the front bench. "She's not going to stab you in the back, Ginshai. Worry about my knife, not hers."

The statement wasn't truthful, just banter between friends. They continued ribald comments, and even Lensu jumped in as the caravan ambled onto the main street of Tose. I envied such casual and true friendship.

I would return to the dank caverns of the Aegis monastery where we were to consider ourselves siblings. We had no such familial connections even if we did not have as many political designs as other sects. I lived in such a cold and emotionless place that I only felt alive when I acted a character to facilitate my assassinations. I did so now, joining in with the jokes.

When we passed under the gates of the city and the guards gave casual inspection, our cajoling subdued but didn't cease. I appeared to pay no notice.

Make sure we are not followed, Khimmer. Guards were not my only threat. Spies would make good coin to spot Queen Meihlia's First Assassin.

Yes, Mistress.

The dirt road leading from the city made for a slow pace and bumpy ride through fresh air and verdant farms. It would lead to the city of Madaea, where the travel routes divided into three directions: sunward to the shore, darkward and north to the snowy peaks which blocked the sun from the land, and the most traveled road to Vale Aganor. I would meet my Aegis contact in Madaea and decide whether to continue with this guise in the caravan or plan another route.

My mission had been successful, and for the moment, I could play the part of a friendly traveler. I'd escaped.

The Silari traveled through the day, and I imagined myself happily part of their group. The farms had disappeared, leaving tree-dotted plains of tan grass. When we stopped to prepare lunch, they arranged the wagons in a partial circle around a low fire.

I opted to join those staying in the carts to watch the horizon. Partially I did so to avoid lying further about the character that I played. I also felt a sadness growing as I watched people who lived as friends and true companions. Eleven Silari took to their tasks; some stood watch, watered and fed horses, or prepared our meal while they enjoyed each other's company. I stared silently across a pale horizon.

Sinda laughed loudly among them and sent young Lensu to bring me a warm plate of spiced grains dotted with poultry and beans. Thin bread served as a utensil. The Silari preferred sharp spices that warmed the tongue. I'd grown fond of their food when I'd been sent to their land to kill a Mindarin shipper hiding from my Queen.

We are being approached, Mistress.

Khimmer's thought provided me with direction, and I lowered my food to turn. I should not have been looking toward the sun side, where our sun hung in its place just over the treetops, but I pointed and called out, "Riders."

Pulling my blade, a short sword on its own, I leaped off the wagon to join the others. I could feign a mild knowledge of weapons and engage in a defense. The Aegis monks had trained me to moderate my proficiency with weapons if I were in a covert position.

Eight riders approached. Toward the rear, I could make out one archer with a crossbow in hand and two others beside her who had bows strapped to their backs.

The Silari produced their own weapons, and two of them took positions under the wagons with crossbows readied.

I rested my left hand on my belt. *Plumbata*, I thought to Khimmer.

Yes, Mistress. I sensed their reluctance. They did not like losing any of Nightarmor, and a dart might not be recovered.

The red-vested man did not draw a weapon, but carried a simple staff as he walked forward to meet the riders.

I circled to the side where the woman with the crossbow would arrive. The Silari were silent while hooves thudded on the field.

The new arrivals wore leather jerkins, and their right forearms had intricate tattoos. They were far from their homes on the sunside shores of Dallobese.

Their leader gestured for the other riders to stop while she continued on, circling her horse to a sweating stance before the Silari leader. "Welcome, travelers, to our small piece of the Madaean highway." She spoke in Dallobese with an obvious threat to her tone.

The Silari leader tapped the staff into the grass. "There is no coin for your claim."

I focused on the woman with the crossbow; she hadn't raised it yet, but her right arm tensed. There would be violence, and I did not want any of the Silari to die.

"Turn back then, Silari, if you have no coin." The horse-woman leaned down, masking her hand reaching for her sword. "We could just take it all."

My target lifted her arm at her leader's signal, and I threw left-handed before starting to run. I didn't aim for her arm, but her thigh spread on the saddle. My weapon sunk deep, and her bow sang without finding a target. She screamed the moment after and yanked out Nightarmor's weapon.

I'd caught the eyes of her companions on my side as I raced toward them. *Hidden armor,* I thought to Khimmer.

Nightarmor flowed to cover my chest and groin where

the simple artisan's smock could hide it. The Silari were known for their tough defense, but I wanted them uninjured.

The leader of the riders swung at the red-vested Silari, but the wooden staff spun and rang the steel. Before I reached my first rider, the red-vested Silari had unhorsed the woman.

Silari crossbows found two marks while I focused on a man turning his steed toward me and brandishing a sword.

Crossing to the side opposite his blade, I tucked under the poor animal's chin and tapped the point of my blade into the front of its leg. The metal touched bone with barely any muscle cut. I passed them as the horse reared.

The Silari left me a lone bowman in the rear to attack with a similar maneuver. His arrow flew back toward the caravan before he belatedly noted my advance. The horse snapped at me before I tapped bone on its foreleg. I hated harming animals. As the archer slid off its rearing mount, I pulled back so they could consider an escape.

My hosts barely noticed my attacks on the riders as the brightly colored merchants closed in. The rider's leader managed to return to her horse, rein in the beast, and ride through Ginshai. She appeared to have taken a nasty gash on her calf.

I found my bloodied plumbata and stepped on it so Nightarmor could reabsorb it. Feigning shock, I crouched as the riders retreated leaving two dead, one wounded running after them, and a new horse for the Silari. *Remove armor.*

Yes, Mistress.

My pulse beat steadily, if a little fast, and sweat trickled under my arms.

Sinda whistled and motioned me back toward the

wagons. "Foolish, running at them with a short blade. You could have been killed."

I acted chagrined. "I was so scared, I couldn't help it."

"Hades take them." She spit in the direction of one of the dead. "Bandits."

I sheathed my blade clumsily, as if shaken. This had been a role I'd played many times. I didn't like deceiving the Silari, but what choice did I have? Traveling along the trade routes always proved dangerous, and contriving my way into groups offered protection and anonymity.

Soon, I would be meeting my Aegis contact, and we would plan for my return home. In another life, I would have preferred to stay with the Silari.

CHAPTER 3

Tallahassee - Earth

I moped on Tyler's bed with a half-read book while they typed furiously at their desk. For the past three days, I'd returned to where I'd seen the tall-eared person, but they hadn't returned.

"Zan just opened a hornet's nest with this troll." Tyler swore. "He needs to move on."

My understanding of English faltered when they ranted about the internet. I knew of Zan, Tyler's friend, but I ignored the rest of their comments. The few times I'd asked for clarification, the explanation had been long and complicated enough that I regretted ever opening my mouth.

When I didn't respond, Tyler glanced over. "Still planning on going out on your vigil this afternoon? I can give you a ride."

"Maybe not. As you said, I likely scared them away." My lips tightened. "You don't believe what I saw, do you?"

Tyler stopped typing and shrugged with one shoulder.

"I mean, you wouldn't lie. But they didn't have tall ears. I was there. What can I say?"

I was naïve about Earth, but I knew what I'd seen. "Have you ever heard about someone like who I'm describing? Maybe on the internet."

"Of course. Aliens on television shows. Elves in stories. That's why I thought you were describing someone in cosplay." Tyler swiveled to face me. "They aren't real, though. If the fairy folk were among us, we'd have pictures by now."

I brightened. My phone had a camera. I would try that next time I found one of the tall-eared people. "I should have taken a picture. Then you'd believe me."

Tyler smiled. "I'm sure that man will love that if you ever catch up to him. But if the stories are true, their glamour likely wouldn't work against cameras."

Glamour, Khimmer?

Attractive, possibly sexual, Mistress.

That made no sense. The man had been handsome enough, but how would that hide his ears? "Glamour? I don't understand."

"Fae magic. They can hide among humans because of their ability to sway the human mind. I think I've got an urban fantasy book downstairs with that kind of magic in it. We'll grab it on the way out." Tyler leaned forward, pleased.

I'd never fully understood the Earth concept of magic, except it could be akin to the powers of the gods and goddesses of Duruce. "Would my truthsense work against that kind of magic?"

Tyler frowned. They knew of my origins, my truthsense, and my Nightarmor, but they seemed uncomfortable talking about the latter two. "I suppose." Tilting back into their chair, they shook their head. "That's creepy. The idea that there might actually be humanoid cryptids."

Cryptids, Khimmer?

I'm guessing non-humans from context, Mistress.

Excitement flushed my cheeks. "That's it then. I can see these other people with my truthsense. I'll get a picture for you." I dropped the book and slid out my phone. "How do I use the camera?"

No wonder the man had been upset. He had been trying to hide from humans, and I'd exposed his secret. I'd be more careful. We could be friends. He *had* been sort of cute.

Tyler motioned for me to lower my phone. A smile played at the edge of their lips. "You look excited."

"I'll prove to you they exist." It had dismayed me that Tyler hadn't seen the ears. They were my first friend, and I wanted them to be part of everything. I'd get them a picture if I needed to spend every day looking for the tall-eared person.

CHAPTER 4

My Aegis contact was waiting for me when the Silari caravan reached the tall buildings of the city of Madaea.

The streets droned with the bustle of carts and the dense throng of humanity packed within the city walls. The heavy scents of horse and human mingled with the spicy cooking from the sidewalk vendors. I longed for the steamed noodles the city was famous for.

My agent, long-haired Hentek, sat at a café located close to the gates. He wore a blue Dallobese merchant robe, leaned back on his chair, and sipped at a white mug.

I ran two fingers over my eyebrow to signify that I'd seen him. The Silari would likely bring their caravan to the city's fairgrounds as they shunned the merchant inns and fixed markets. The streets were familiar enough that I could make my way back to him, though he'd likely have to drink a cup or two.

Ginshai swore at two street urchins running between

the caravans, and Sinda smacked his arm. The Silari's easy-going nature had returned quickly after the raider attack. I'd hidden a darker mood partially brought on by the skirmish, but more so out of envy for their deep friendships.

As expected, we pulled onto the fairgrounds, and the red-vested man negotiated with one of the attendants.

I pulled out my bag and jumped to the grass. "I want to buy some noodles; how long will you be here?"

Sinda eyed my pack, but likely thought me just cautious. "Overnight, usually. We need to get a healer, so maybe two nights."

"That's enough time for me to eat." I laughed, but she had answered all I needed to know. If Hentek felt the road straight to Vale Aganor was safe, then I would continue with the Silari. Perhaps after I bought some noodles.

I strolled with ease through a city known for its rougher neighborhoods. The safer, more heavily traveled streets had merchants in booths or shops to take your coin and pick-pockets milling in the crowds. Since I kept my coin inside Nightarmor's belt, no one found mine.

The disguised Aegis monk sipped chocolate as I sat at the table next to him and ordered a black tea I favored. The server left, and Hentek held his cup before his lips. "The high pass is favored."

I groaned quietly. Toward the dark side, the temperature grew cold, and between here and up to Vale Aganor, mountains crested with snow. Miners and herders traveled the routes there, but few traders or caravans. I'd likely be walking most of the way.

"Word of Kloro has reached Madaea. They blame the Queen."

I had left nothing to incriminate Queen Meihlia. There had been no Blessed Blade of Nyx. The rumor had to be started in reaction to Kloro's own actions in avoiding her tax. All merchants knew that was a risky endeavor. His death had been a reminder.

Hentek finished his chocolate, placed a coin beside the empty cup, and stood. "Night's blessing," he said.

Peripherally, I watched him leave to see if anyone else followed. I'd never understood the Aegis blessing as the only night was perpetually on the dark side of Duruce. We'd need more than a blessing to survive in those temperatures.

When the server brought my tea, I engaged her in a light-hearted conversation about the best steamed noodles in the city. I intended a warm meal before I bought supplies for the trip. Dallobese highlanders were reclusive, and I'd likely find it quiet on the road toward the dark side.

It would be many mornings before I reached home, and no bells would call the time. I had Khimmer to measure our trip, though.

CHAPTER 5

Highlands, close to the dark side of Duruce

My cloak flapping in the strong winds, I stepped to the top of a low ridge along the trail and crouched. *Khimmer, can you identify?*

The gray cliffs to my right merged into the black mountain range bordering the dark side. Below me, the trail curved beside rock walls down to a waterfall and river which flowed away into the lower hills. A cluster of people scrambled at a crevice cut by the water. Their erratic movements spoke of distress.

Five people, Mistress. Three adults and two children, one of whom is in the water.

A child?

Yes, Mistress.

My pulse rose. I had avoided the only other people along this trail since yesterday morning. My mentor would chastise my actions, but I could not ignore a child in danger. I started forward in an easy downhill lope.

There were two women and a young girl in the fur-lined leathers common to the region. A man leaned over the edge of the crevice, glistening with water and stripped to his tunic and pants.

Light and tight under, toe and thumb spikes, no helmet, I thought to Khimmer.

Under my thick wool jerkin, sleeved tunic, and pants, Nightarmor poured over my skin in a thin metal more akin to mail than plate. My trail led to a set of split logs closer to the waterfall.

I unclasped my hooded robe as the older woman caught sight of me. She had gray hair braided down her neck. The tattoo of the goddess Phylloa marked her jaw by the ear. An already worried expression turned tight with fierce concern.

"How can I help?" I asked, more to assuage her concerns than to assume they had any plans.

The man looked up, his face scraped and bleeding. "My son."

I dropped cloak, supplies, and water with three steps to come to a perch on the ravine's edge.

The water pounded in a roar to my right, but the force of it continued into a gully it had worn. White foam splashed from ledge to ledge out of sight.

The young boy was wedged against the torrent in the rocks. No more than ten, he had enough strength and sense to lock himself there with both feet while one gloved hand pressed against the water-covered ledge.

Kneeling, I inspected the wall below me. There were few cracks, as most of the shape had been driven by water. What bottom I could see had been worn smooth. The boy was beyond reach.

The younger woman gasped as I rolled off the ledge.

The older woman studied me and especially Nightarmor's gloves.

My feet splashed into cold water. At the edge of the dark side, rivers were born from the constant snowstorms in the darkness.

Khimmer threw spikes out my heels as the current slid my right foot. With my left thumb claw in a crack, I shuffled closer to the boy. "I'm going to lift you to your father. When I have a good grip, you have to release. Understand?"

Water spraying on his face, he chanced an open eye and blinked. I sensed fear in the change of expression. How many strangers did they see here? He winced and didn't answer.

As I stretched my hand out, my right heel scraped and released from the unrelenting pressure. The shift in my body's position loosened my left thumb's hold.

Mistress, may I recommend a helmet?

Later. If I go over the edge. I didn't need to give these people anything more to talk about. They were isolated, but not alone. Besides, I'd need a bulkier armor to survive the next drop in the rolling water. The ledge below looked to be nearly twice my height.

Dragging my right heel slowly back, a spike clicked into a crack, and I put my weight down. The curved spike found purchase.

I forced out a breath to calm myself, shoved my right thumb spike into a deep crack, and released the grip with my left hand. The roar covered whatever they yelled from above. The boy peeked out through drenched slits, but seemed hopeful.

His leather coat provided a good grip, and he followed my earlier instruction as I wrenched him up.

The father had taken off his gloves, and both women knelt at his legs, pinning him.

My right foot gave out from under me. Flinging the boy as high as I could, I scrambled to regain a hold with my toe spike.

The boy's weight released, I slammed my left hand to join my right. Luckily, the thumb spike found the same crack. Both of my legs flew out from under me and shot off the ledge with the flow of water.

The falls splashed at my dangling heels, begging me to join them. Khimmer had strengthened Nightarmor at my thumbs, so that despite the twisting angle, I felt little of the pressure. My heart raced, and I took a deep breath through gritted teeth. Water pounded the rocks with a constant roar and sprayed against the left side of my face.

The flow resisted any attempt to simply pull my feet to the ledge. Without looking, I scraped my right toe up the side. A click vibrated through the armor, and I tested a foot hold. It held. Trailing my left foot even higher along the rocks, I managed to pin against a smooth lip.

I turned up to my hands to find the boy gone and the man reaching down for me. There was a good arm's length distance between my highest grip and his waiting fingers.

Shaking my head, I pulled my right foot loose and searched for purchase at the ledge, where the current was the strongest. Each step and change in handhold threatened to reset my progress or toss me into the white foam.

It took a series of careful maneuvers before I let him grab my arm. The jerkin tore as he pulled me over rock, but I sighed when my knee crossed over the edge. We toppled back.

We smiled and laughed together, but there were tears in his eyes.

The mother had wrapped the child in her own leather coat and offered me a weak smile. "Thanks to you and the goddess." She spoke in a tight-throated whisper.

The older woman still studied me with a tight face. "We need to hurry before the cold sets in." She motioned back in the direction I'd just come. "The fire will stoke quickly."

I moved for my belongings strewn on the rock and collected my dry cloak first.

Detach gloves.

Yes, Mistress.

I felt Nightarmor separate at my wrists. Carefully, so the older woman could see, I peeled off the gloves and placed them in my cloak even though they were only wet on the outside.

The father shook as he placed a heavy hand on my shoulder. "Thank you."

"I had to try. I'm glad he's okay. Your son?" The wind ripped through my wet jerkin and tunic.

He nodded. "My only."

From the dry pocket of the cloak, I took my fur-lined leather gloves. From the older woman's expression, she still did not appear to trust me. A deep chill had sunk to my bones, and it would not end until we reached somewhere warm. Water had soaked my hair, and the cloak's cowl did little to warm me.

The older woman took the lead and glanced back as she departed from the main path. Her eyes caught mine immediately.

I recognized the trail up to their lands. I'd passed it just a short while before.

"Quick," the older woman said. Despite her white hair, she kept a strong pace uphill.

Goats and sheep called from pens on a rocky farm of

tough grass and few short trees. Their house was a common highlander mud and stone construct with a sod roof. Indeed, thin smoke trailed out the chimney.

The older woman entered before us, and an oil lantern sputtered to life as I closed the door behind me. The oil mixed with the musty odor of people and burnt fires.

"Get out of those wet clothes," the old woman said.

I nodded and turned, opening my cloak wide. Remove armor, Khimmer.

The man and I peeled off clothes while the mother took sodden clothes off her shivering son. The daughter talked lightly of the incident while she worked with the older woman to find cloaks and blankets to dry and warm us while they built up the fire. The mother spoke quietly in soothing tones.

The older woman inspected the bangles, choker, and bracelets of Nightarmor that I wore, then handed me a woolen blanket of bright reds and yellows. Her accent was thick. "You are not highlander. What purpose sets you on these trails?" She didn't ask my name, but struck straight to the heart of why I crossed their land.

I pulled the wool tight around me and shuffled closer to the hearth. "I have a sister who has married a highlander man, up across the Vale Aganor border. I've never had the chance to visit, and my troupe is resting for a bit in Madaea. I'd not imagined the roads so rough up here."

She snorted. "Still. You've done my niece well by saving the boy. We've food and a warm hearth to rest. I'd like to tell the future for one such as you." Her lips turned up at the corners, nearly a smile. "Yes, I'd like that."

The father already had the daughter fetching drink while he placed a cooking pot over the fire. The single room had heated quickly and fought the chill in my bones.

I tried to ignore the offer of a foretelling; the high-landers and some of the sunside islanders favored the practice. I'd heard there were those who could truly see, but had yet to meet one. The two times I'd spent coin on the practice, I was to be wed within days and pregnant soon afterward. I would never be wed as a member of the Aegis order. Careful with proper herbs, I'd be as likely pregnant. I wondered if perhaps they had sensed Khimmer.

Mother and father thanked me repeatedly while we talked, as if unsure what else to say to me, and I'd thought to finally curl up for sleep when the older woman, the aunt, sat beside me. "Lay your head in my lap."

I shook my head, not wanting to offend her. "You've already warmed me and fed me, more than is necessary."

She didn't speak, but that sly smile crept up again as she grabbed my shoulders and turned me. I would have had to jerk away not to be placed down, looking up into her face. Her skin was cold and wrinkled as she placed two fingers at the side of my neck and three on my forehead.

"Breathe," she commanded.

I hadn't intended on not, but took deeper, longer breaths.

She began whispering and singing a chant that repeated but used no words.

Do you recognize it? I asked Khimmer.

No, Mistress.

The room had quieted, as if the family knew to give us silence. The only sounds came from the girl fidgeting, the buffeting wind, and the crackle of the fire.

I could have slept it took so long, but I didn't.

When the aunt spoke her eyes popped open, startling me. "You will travel where only the goddesses and gods have been, and forsaken.

"Where you go, you will find others who conceal their lies, but they will not be able to hide from you.

"Your worth, your abilities, and your possessions shall be another's obsession, risking those who stand beside you, yet none will survive if you stand alone.

"A child shall deceive you, and unless you question yourself, you might be lost.

"Her sleeping son shall repair what you have broken.

"May your tongue become your sword if you would save them."

She pushed me away from her as if I were to be avoided.

I sat up, grabbed my braid, and tried to make sense of her ramblings, but couldn't. At least, I wasn't going to be pregnant.

CHAPTER 6

Railroad Square Art District, Tallahassee - Earth

A number of times, Tyler drove me to the same location at the right time, but the tall-eared man never returned. I gave up searching for him. It was a score of days later when Deanna brought me to the Railroad Square Art District in Tallahassee.

"Amazing, aren't they?" Deanna pointed at the murals covering the large metal walls of a warehouse. People had painted the sides of all the buildings that made up the diverse neighborhood. The secluded community hung heavy with the aroma of cooking food tainted with city exhaust. It didn't look like other parts of Tallahassee, and the people seemed more relaxed. I liked it.

Deanna had brought me shopping to a store the size of a small market, which sold an odd variety of used items.

Following Deanna to an art studio, I caught a delicious aroma of cooking. When we'd first arrived, we'd gotten tea and something sweet at a nearby place called the Square Mug. With the smell of hearty food, I became famished.

A red building with a shaded pavilion sat across the street. One half looked like wood, and the other half metal. "I'm hungry." I slowed, and Deanna followed my gaze.

"Pete's cooking is the best. Even Tyler will eat here, and you know how picky they are." She waited for a car to pass. "It's called the Crum Box Gastgarden. They do music and events. We'll eat outside."

I liked the name, but had no idea what it meant. *Translation, Khimmer?*

Unknown, Mistress. A colloquial name of some sort.

The sign had a picture that could have been a train car, and the metal side of the building appeared to be one.

Inside the building smelled even better. Signs and pictures decorated the walls, and behind a polished counter, stairs led up into the train. A smiling man with a beard and kind eyes appeared and dashed down the steps. "Welcome!" He tilted his head at Deanna. "You've been here before." He had an easy way about him.

"Ahnjii's first time." Deanna pointed to me.

"Fresh sausage today." Pete slid two menus in front of us and rattled off some of the beverages available.

I picked out a sandwich. "Fries?" I asked.

He chuckled. "Sorry, no."

Deanna pointed at the menu. "Mac and cheese. It's the best."

We ate delicious food outside where I could watch people walking about Railroad Square. Occasionally the city noise around us would intrude, but in this little section, Tallahassee felt peaceful. Deanna chatted about the other stores and galleries we'd visit.

Pete bounced out of the building to check on us and

nodded with satisfaction at the empty plates and containers. "All good out here?"

"I love the food," I told him. "Can I come back?" I asked Deanna.

She laughed and smiled at Pete. "We'll be back for sure."

Pete grinned. "Thanks for the warning."

I liked him. Imagining living nearby and being able to stop in for mac and cheese anytime made me smile.

"I've got to show you some clothes. They're not your style, but they could be." Deanna stood, and I followed.

We were walking to another shop when I spotted one of the tall-eared people.

Dressed more like Deanna than myself, the woman had blonde hair, pastel clothes, dangling jewelry, and tall ears. Easily my age, she climbed a set of short steps and entered a door.

I stopped. My pulse raced.

"C'mon. Don't stand in the street." Deanna paused, patting her hair as she looked up and down the road.

I pointed at the row of colorful buildings where the tall-eared woman had entered, in the opposite direction from where Deanna had been leading us. "I want to go in there. I'll meet you." Without looking, I gestured generally toward the stores where we'd been heading.

"Okay." Deanna sounded disappointed.

"I'm sorry." I took off with slow strides. The last time I'd scared the tall-eared man, but now I understood why. Humans on Earth couldn't see the ears. We had no such people on Duruce that I knew of, and I couldn't ignore an opportunity.

The first door led to a second with a warning about cats

being inside. I thought it odd, but stepped in and smelled both books and cats immediately.

She looked up from the counter with an easy smile. "Welcome to Fat Cat Books. Have you been here before?"

I shook my head and grinned. "No."

As I hoped, she approached to explain. I was determined not to scare her away. Waiting until she finished giving a description of the business and their goals, I pointed to myself. "My name's Ahnjii."

Tyler and Deanna had both said that I was personable and easy to get along with. I hoped that would work today.

"Vivianne," she said. "We've got Jenny, a calico; would you like to see her?"

"Yes."

There wasn't much more than two aisles of books, one with chairs and tables where two cats lounged. A black cat peeked at us from the top of a bookshelf.

Vivianne sat on one side of a multi-colored cat and scratched along its jaw. "She's about a year old and very sweet."

I needed to bring about the topic slowly. "She's got big ears."

Vivianne furrowed her eyebrows. "I suppose she does. She's young."

I stroked the cat's fur along her back the way Jake and Willie, Deanna's tabbies, liked it. A subtle comment was needed to discuss Vivianne's ears. However, she took my petting of the cat to mean the end of our discussion. Vivianne started to rise.

"You've got tall ears," I said both quietly and a bit hastily. My already fast pulse started to race.

Vivianne, already lifted from the chair, knocked it over.

The cat under my fingers darted away, and the room burst into scurrying felines.

My hand tightened on my braid. "I'm sorry, I didn't know how to bring it up." I'd ruined it, but she hadn't run out the front door. Still, my heart pounded.

Her long fingers straight, Vivianne sucked in a breath. "You can see them?" She glanced at a back door before she dropped her voice. "Past a sigil?"

Sigil?

A symbol, Mistress, magical according to one of Tyler's books.

I shrugged. "I guess so."

"Do the other witches know? Have you told them what you see?" Vivianne closed her eyes. "You must have."

I knew the term, but I wasn't a witch. "No, I told Tyler, but they don't believe me." The cats had calmed, and I rose slowly, wanting to right the chair. "I'm not a witch."

Vivianne's face tightened. "You are. I could sense you when you came in. A very strong empath, I had thought to myself. I was sure you'd sensed me as well. Yet, you did act strangely." Her forehead creased, but she didn't frown.

I remembered a witch as being a scary person who threatened children, though I couldn't remember the story exactly.

Empath?

Unknown, Mistress.

Vivianne hadn't lied to me; my truthsense would have let me know that. She truly thought I was a witch and empath.

We stood quiet for a moment. She had calmed somewhat and only pulled back a step when I righted the chair. "I'm sorry. I didn't mean to scare you. I just wanted to meet you. What are you?"

She shook her head as if exasperated. "You are a very strange witch. I'm Fae, as you well know. Perhaps you should leave."

As she pointed for the front door, my chest felt hollow. I hadn't meant for this to go so wrong. The term Fae meant nothing to me, but I didn't care. "Please help me understand. I'm new here."

I held my breath. Tyler had been clear not to let anyone know that I was from someplace other than Earth. Early on, Deanna had told me not to mention it as well, but she didn't believe me.

"What is there to understand? I'm more at risk here than you when you tell others. All Fae are. I don't know what the high Fae will do."

She hadn't understood that I'd meant new to Earth. I had learned the name of her people, but I didn't understand the high Fae difference. "I won't tell anyone."

Vivianne frowned. "Why not?"

"You're asking me to protect your identity and secrets. Why wouldn't I honor that? I don't want you hurt from something I do, even if I don't understand." I stepped back toward my seat, hoping she'd relax and sit with me. At least, she no longer pointed at the door.

This promise meant that I couldn't tell Tyler, but if they knew what was being asked, they would understand. It also meant no photographs.

She studied me. Her expression had relaxed, but I could tell she mulled over the situation. The multi-colored cat strolled back from the bookshelves and rubbed against my leg.

"You've never met a Fae before?"

I chuckled. "I didn't know he was Fae, but I did

approach someone with tall ears on the street. It went worse than this did."

Vivianne fought a smile. "I imagine. I was ready to run."

We both jumped when the front door opened. Deanna, a bag swinging from her hand, stepped inside. "Hi, Kitty!"

A gray tabby waved its tail and sauntered ahead of her.

"I've never been in here. Getting some books?" Deanna passed the bookshelf and looked over to Vivianne. "Hello. Ooh, a calico." Deanna tilted her head at me. "I want to get back; Tyler said they were making lunch. I didn't tell them we ate. They seemed excited, and I didn't want to disappoint them. You ready?"

I turned back to Vivianne. "I want to hang out here for a while. I can walk back."

Vivianne did not argue the point or even look distressed. I suppressed a grin.

Deanna sighed. "Are you sure? It's hot today."

Both she and Tyler were always surprised when I offered to walk. Khimmer would direct me, and I didn't feel we were that far away.

"I'll be fine." I couldn't be sure how much Vivianne would tell me about her people, but just talking with her was exciting.

"Your choice. It'll give me a chance to put off a second lunch." Deanna smiled at the calico, then waved at Vivianne. "Lovely place. I'll be back sometime."

As Deanna headed for the door, I slowly sat in my chair, hoping Vivianne would join me. She remained standing, but leaned against the bookshelf.

She spoke as Deanna closed the front door. "She's not a witch."

"I don't think so."

"You'd be able to tell. I can tell."

"I live with her and her sibling, Tyler. Her boyfriend stays there too."

"Not witches?" Vivianne asked.

I shrugged. "Never thought to ask."

"You'd know, and they would have said something." Vivianne leaned forward, her eyes widening. "You've never lived with witches, not even family?"

"I'm an orphan." I wasn't about to mention that I'd been raised with Aegis monks, but I hadn't killed my parents until just before I'd accidentally gotten myself marooned on Earth. I trusted Tyler's judgment that I shouldn't expose that information.

CHAPTER 7

Vale Aganor - Duruce

I strode dutifully downslope toward Vale Aganor. The wildlife bustled in the forest to each side, and hidden birds chirped happily. The broad roofs of the city peeked between breaks in green canopy. Looming and black, Mount Ergus rose above all; it had been visible since I exited the darkward mountains.

The Queen's castle of white marble clung to the sunward side of the sharp cliffs, a stark contrast to the black rock. From this angle I could see the hints of window arches, balconies, and parapets.

I kept pace behind a shepherd and his teenage daughter leading a small flock on the road. She sang a light-hearted tune for their charges, so her notes only reached me on occasion. Their flock's scent was far more noticeable.

The forest dwindled far ahead of them, and golden wheat fields stretched across farms. The sun hung just over the golden dome of Oyzys and seemed to set fire to the curved edges.

I did love Vale Aganor. The streets were clean, and the guard kept peace under Queen Meihlia. Even the rowdiest sections where the taverns circled the fairgrounds yielded little more than bloody noses. Artisans' children ran freely, often hawking wares when they remembered. Yet, my mood had turned dark. I blamed it on the trip with Silari. Their camaraderie blazed light on the shade of my empty life.

Despite the dire warnings of the Aegis monks, Turben especially, I needed some friendship.

The farms pulled back the veil of the forests and exposed Vale Aganor stretching from the Queen's castle and the slopes of Mount Ergus. Brightly colored houses marked the outer limits of the city, black and white roofs glinted with the sun, and golden domes and spires rose above them all. Unlike the walled-in city of Madaea, Vale Aganor spoke of gentleness. Without my skills as an assassin, the labors of my fellow Aegis monks, and the Queen's renowned benevolence, we might have the misfortune to fear soldiers and war. I should not be so glum.

The dusty trail turned to cobblestone at the corner of two short houses; both had side porches with children and small kitchen gardens, but one was painted blue with yellow trim while the other was dark pink and red. Each time I arrived in Vale Aganor from the darkward road, I imagined the families who lived inside and the meals they sat down to enjoy after the evening bells.

Mistress, is something wrong?

I sucked in a breath at Khimmer's thought. They rarely commented on my mood unless it threatened my work. Losing my frown, I thought, *Petulant, Turben would call it.*

I'm feeling sorry for myself. Ignore it. I'll get past it. I always did.

I smiled to the children and turned the corner, joining the light traffic of the street. The Queen's castle rose six stories high ahead of me. As if the light marble had been carved from Mount Ergus itself, the towers and parapets sunk deep into black cliffs. Flags rustled and banners fluttered. I forced pride to push away my self-pity and strode with a studied spring to my step.

My mood had lightened by the time I reached the back of the temple of Gerais and started up the wide stairs of the Queen's castle. I recognized one of the guards in their red and white-trimmed uniforms. I'd bedded him in one of the lower taverns a few months back. His smile said he recognized me.

"A highlander shepherd?" he asked me. He'd trimmed his beard short along a square jaw and shaved the cheeks.

I skipped up the last step, arms out in display. In truth, I couldn't wait to get out of the heavy cold-weather clothes. The fur inside was too hot and stunk of sweat. "Sold my flock and ready to spend my coin in shining Vale Aganor." I couldn't remember the guard's name.

He winked. "Try the Copper Kettle by the fairgrounds. I'll be there tonight."

I gave the other guard, an older man with gray in his goatee, a flashing smile and scampered between them into the grand arch of carved marble. Perhaps I would take the guard up on his offer. I could use a release. However, my evening schedule rested in the hands of Turben more than my own.

Inside the doors of the castle, the sprawling entryway had two gilded stairs leading up to a guarded arch ahead. Under and between the steps sat a dark alcove where I would be heading down to the Aegis monastery. Our quarters were carved under the castle and deep into Mount Ergus. My boots echoed in the hall, and potted shrubs flowered with a heady scent.

"Ahnjii." A woman's voice called from the curve of the stairs. Her shoes clacked methodically down the steps, and her left hand trailed along the rail. Her light beige dress draped a graceful curtsy on each step. "You've returned. I will assume successfully."

Gigina, Ambassador to Tahnet, was also my adviser on many of the cultures outside Vale Aganor. An older woman, she wore her white hair up and decorated it with tiny jewels.

As I paused and smiled, my own scent, musky and sharp from traveling, overpowered the blossoms. I would discuss my mission with Turben, but Gigina had not asked a direct question. "I'm glad to be home." The last word tugged at my expression.

"Of course, nothing more beautiful than shining Vale Aganor." She stepped down the last three steps and buried her lie. "Except of course, the golden halls of Helios."

Truth. At least the last statement; the first had been a casual lie common with nobles and members of the Queen's retinue.

"You must have just returned yourself." After the Ambassador had begun her annual trip to Tahnet, I had left on my mission.

"Yesterday. We should have tea and compare tales."

I blinked in surprise. Shifting the straps of my burdens, I ran my fingers down my braid and pulled it forward. "Tea?"

Our relationship had always been of student and teacher. This sounded like a social engagement. I studied her face. Could this be a possible friend? She already lived at risk. Ambassadors were often evading assassinations. They were targets for one rival to disrupt the relations of two countries. I would not be putting her in any danger she did not already experience.

"Yes. My quarters. I have a wonderful view from my balcony. You've long outgrown our studies, and we barely see each other, except for a chance meeting in the hall." She paused just an arm's length away and wrinkled her nose. "Perhaps tomorrow after midday bells? It'll give you time to freshen up."

I laughed, not exactly embarrassed. "Sounds fun. I'll need to see what Turben has planned for me."

"Sparring, I would guess." Gigina pulled out a delicate bone fan and nodded toward the soldiers at the arch above. "Send word tomorrow morning if you can make it. I'll need to prepare."

I nodded and turned toward the inset alcove of the Aegis monastery. My darker mood had vanished with the simple thought of a quiet meeting. I drank with the guards often enough, but we all knew I couldn't be friends. Gigina might be the perfect opportunity for me.

I pulled open the heavy wooden door and let it thud behind me. I stepped down dark, rough-hewn stairs. Dread rose in my chest. The silence ahead amplified each tap of Nightarmor's heel on rock.

Flickering lantern light played on the stone walls as if lurid figures danced.

I assumed Turben would already know I'd arrived and would be waiting in his room. Each step I took a little faster, hoping it would expedite my report and get me to the baths.

The cool, stale air did little to cover my odor, even as the stairs ended in a wide, dark corridor. The ceiling disappeared into pitch black where monks with crossbows waited on ledges out of sight. The one lantern across from the steps lit me easily enough, but the hall stretched into darkness to both sides. Lights waited farther along, but each hall had long stretches of darkness.

I skipped to the left. What would having tea be like in the castle? Gigina would likely have it all proper with nice chairs and Mindarin china teacups. It felt peculiar and exciting compared to a mug of ale at a tavern with random guards or a cup at a café while meeting a contact.

"Ahnjii. My Shadow." A low voice spoke lightly from the darkness.

Turben. My expression disappeared, and I lifted my head to face him, placing my left hand on my right wrist. "My Shadow. I have returned."

"Yes." A single foot intentionally scraped the floor. "Follow."

We headed away from Turben's room, passing the stairs I'd come down. Where was he taking me? I drew in a deep breath of the musty cavern air. The kitchens and the refectory were in this direction, so perhaps he thought I was hungry. Trotting, I kept up to his pace.

"Where are we going?" I asked.

Turben didn't answer. As we passed a lantern, I glanced over at his face of angular edges and sharp shadows. He knew I was looking at him, but didn't turn toward me. His expression gave no hint to his mood, as usual.

We continued toward the hall that housed the various arenas. Natural caverns had been worked to smooth floors. Dull grunts echoed from the openings ahead.

"We're sparring?" I had planned on explaining my report quietly, sitting on the floor of his room.

"You've been gone for eight evening bells." There was no hint of what he felt or what his purpose was.

I rolled my shoulders forward, already stretching muscles. Maybe I stunk bad enough that he'd keep it short. His feet were bare, prepared to spar.

The training room Turben chose had a pit in the center with wooden equipment against the natural walls. Braziers burned close to the edge of the empty circle of sand. Three cloaked Aegis monks worked unarmed against wooden poles and weighted bags. They did not glance at us, but each had surely noted our entry.

With a sigh, I began to remove my water and supplies. I paused when Turben pushed me toward the shallow pit.

"An ambush. No time to prepare." He gave me a second shove when we reached the short lip.

My boots dug into the sand clumsily, putting me off balance. I managed to spin, heaving my satchel into the air. It caught Turben's right arm with a light thud from my mentor's punch. His left palm slammed into my sternum.

I rolled backward and gained distance and a quick breath.

"Kloro is dead."

I dove away from his kick, leaving my water bag on the sand. "In his crapper."

Turben's strike for my throat came as expected, but I blocked. When he followed with his leg sweep I leaned into it, toppled backward onto the sand, and rolled sideways. He managed a kick to my shoulder, but I'd left my supplies at his feet.

"You improvised. I could tell by the description of the wounds."

I feigned a block and managed a glancing kick on his

elbow. Smiling, I hopped away. "What man pees sitting down?"

Turben's silent response landed two kicks to my side, a dizzying fist to my head, and a neck strike that would have broken my windpipe if he'd not tempered the punch.

"I improvised. I took the best available shot." My kick clipped his hip, but I had to scurry to avoid the backlash. My left side ached, and I kept shaking my head to focus. With two carefully maneuvered dodges, I threw off the heavy coat.

"Wrong choice." He struck and I blocked. His left hand wrapped around my forearm. Instead of pulling away, I jumped high into him, bringing my knee up quickly.

He'd planned for the move and swung me sideways. I hit hard enough that my elbow found the bottom of the sand and pain trailed up to my wrist.

I sprang up and away from his next strike. "He would have been warned and taken precautions. It would have delayed . . ."

Turben's right fist caught my side. "You didn't want to come back and say you'd failed."

I kept drawing in air as I scuttled backward. Of course I didn't want to fail.

"Silari," Turben said as darted in for a feint.

I blocked his low kicks and tried to grab his forearm when he punched. "Obvious choice. Easy people."

"Consequences?"

"Minor skirmish with raiders." I smiled when I scored a hit on his upper chest, but lost the attempt to grapple his left arm.

His next three hits left me dazed, and my right foot dragged through sand trying to rebound. "Gigina?" Turben caught my ankle and spun me face first into the sand.

As he pinned me down, I sputtered. "She wants to have tea." He'd known about the meeting quicker than I'd expected.

He leaned down to my ear as he gripped me in a choke. "Your response?"

I waited until he released me and jumped clear. "I didn't say no. She's an ambassador." My body ached, and I hoped that his last pin would end the sparring. I pushed up slowly. "Befriending her would not add to her risk."

"Can you see how your emotions control you? You will tell her no. I care nothing for the risk to her, you are correct in that one thing." He didn't even breathe heavily as he exited the sand. "You need to learn to welcome your isolation. Friends are a distraction, and we have a duty."

Anger welled inside me. I should have expected no other response from Turben. Cold and cruel, he cared nothing for living. There would be more to my life. I would have tea with Gigina and suffer the beating that would follow.

After a limping walk back down the halls, I climbed into the tepid bath with a side full of bruises and a painful welt on my cheek darkening the eye. Warm water splashed out of clay pipes protruding from the wall. The moist rock smelled welcoming.

There were two other monks already lathering from the pots of soft soap: a young man I'd never met and an older woman whom I saw regularly. I had bedded her a couple years back. She offered a smile, then frowned at my bruises.

"My Shadow, I thought you were better, from my experience," she said.

Nightarmor had reduced to thick bangles and bracelets and a loose choker for the purpose of the bath. Otherwise naked, my side looked ugly.

I laughed. "Turben felt I needed a lesson."

She smiled knowingly, but the younger man turned sharply at the mention of my mentor's name. He studied my body as I waded closer to the soap pot. Young and fit, he still had some muscle to put on his bones. His eyes followed Nightarmor's jewelry. I sighed and dug out a handful of musky paste to begin lathering.

I think he has the hots for you, Khimmer.

I am unique, being the last, Mistress.

My hair had collected sand from the sparring. It always felt unusual when loose on my shoulders. The swelling on my face stung as I frowned. I knew I wasn't the best assassin and only the Queen's First because of Nightarmor.

Once I'd dried, braided my hair, and dressed in a fresh tunic and trousers, I left the monastery and castle. Turben's rough treatment left me bruised and disappointed. I'd wanted to come home, just not to his attentions.

The evening bells were coming soon, and I wanted to wander Vale Aganor as a reminder of my duty. Most of the shops were closed, and the taverns were starting to crowd with customers. Children played where they could, and their high-pitched, happy voices helped lift my spirits. My profession, hardships, and training gave the Queen the opportunity to avoid the wars that had enveloped our past. An artisan family no longer needed to worry that their children would be sent to kill and die at the borders.

I paused to watch three children playing a jumping game where they tried to gain the longest distance. At their age, I'd been collecting the same bruises I felt today.

A voice louder than the children's called for guards. A second joined and a third, prompting me to jog toward the corner. Metal rang on metal.

An elderly couple had paused on the edge of a side

street, looking back at the next intersection. I could not see what they watched, but the altercation sounded from that direction.

Sheath and blade.

Yes, Mistress.

Nightarmor formed a light vambrace on my left forearm and a sheathed short blade with the hilt at my wrist. I burst into a run just as two red-uniformed guards ran along the cross street. They had their halberds down and in their two hands as if ready to fight.

Someone shouted in Tahni. I recognized the guttural notes, but a thick accent obscured the words. The Tahnet who visited Vale Aganor were usually merchants, but the tone sounded aggressive and a little drunk.

I reached the corner to find three oddly dressed Tahnet brandishing long, curved swords at the two guards. A man lay on the cobblestones bleeding, and a carriage driver was attempting to back up his horses.

One of the Tahnet, a woman taller than any of the others, sliced through the leather glove of one of the guards. He screamed in pain and would have taken a strike to the chest were it not for his comrade's halberd.

Judging her to be the most competent fighter, I raced to place myself between them, calling to Khimmer without pulling my blade. *Full armor and sword.*

Nightarmor poured around me as she swung overhead for my shoulder. Her blade clanged on stiff pauldrons. Through Khimmer's vision I could make out her features, now colored red and orange.

With one guard disabled, it left the other to protect him against the other two Tahnet. Why were they attacking? Surely they knew that more guards would arrive and they would die or be imprisoned.

I reached up for the hilt of Nightarmor's sword that had formed on my back. The woman retreated two steps, her eyes widening. Few saw Nightarmor in action, though many knew of it.

Her hesitation gave me an opening, and I slashed at one of her comrades, a squat man who rained blows against the remaining guard's halberd.

Tahnets with curved swords and strange garb?

Sunward Tahnet sailors, Mistress.

Little of Tahnet had access to the sunside sea, partially because of Vale Aganor's claims. I'd never realized they had sailors. I feigned high and caught his thigh.

The tall woman had recovered and slammed three strikes against my left arm. I worried more for the guards than myself. Only a Blessed Blade could pierce Nightarmor. I could take all three in time, but not guarantee the guards' safety. She jumped clear when I turned my attention back to her.

The Tahnet I'd wounded limped but pressed his attack. I parried a swing with Nightarmor's thin blade and flicked a cut down his forearm.

The man they'd killed bled heavily across the cobblestones. He was a merchant from his clothes. *Why kill him?*

Unknown, Mistress.

The guard beside me cried out and pulled back. Ignoring the woman, I stepped into the two Tahnet men. The one I had wounded moved too slowly, and I slashed deep across his wrist. Blood gushed from him and he stumbled back, his sword clattering to the ground. He lost his footing and dropped to one knee.

The woman's blows rang the side of my helmet as I whipped a slash at the remaining Tahnet man. He expertly blocked me at the last second. Her next blow caught my left elbow and side with such force that I staggered. *Damn me to Hades.* Teeth clenched, I parried with her comrade, ignoring her.

The guard's halberd point drove into the man's neck.

I turned to the woman with a smile. She couldn't see my expression, but I enjoyed watching her gritty determination fade when I let her pound strike after strike into Nightarmor.

"Yield," I said loud enough for her to hear through my helmet. The fight had been somewhat fair when it had been more than her.

She dulled her sword with two more slashes before she gave up. I put my arm out when the guard started around me. The Tahnet woman dropped her weapon to the ground, letting it rattle at her boots. Her voice was low and deep as she muttered in her language.

Translation?

Unclear, Mistress. I believe she is accusing someone of stealing her coin.

As she dropped to her knees, I glanced at the dead merchant down the street. The two Tahnet man were also bleeding on the street. Any exhilaration I'd built during the skirmish ebbed away.

Remove helmet.

Yes, Mistress.

The world shifted back to my normal view as Nightarmor melted off my face. The one Tahnet had already bled out from his neck wound; the second would follow soon, as he'd lost too much blood from his wrist. The street stunk of feces. "Fare well into the house of Hades."

"Don't waste your prayers on these goat lovers," the guard murmured. Boots on the stone behind us told me more guards had arrived.

Four red uniforms swarmed the tall woman, and I shared a glance with her as they pinned her arms behind her back. The two Tahnet men could have been her friends. Had they been joking when they arrived in Vale Aganor? Had they been close like the Silari of the caravan?

Nightarmor protected me. It made me untouchable. I slipped the sword onto my back, and it held.

Remove armor.

Yes, Mistress.

Nyx's gift of truthsense and the ancient armor had made me a tool of the Aegis monks. Untouchable and alone.

The guards were saying something to me when I turned and walked down the street. The three teens who'd been playing and jumping stood with the crowd at the intersection. Their young expressions were mixed between awe and stricken with disgust or fear.

How did I feel? I was hungry. Blood coated the toes of my boots. I felt alone.

No matter what Turben wanted, I would be having tea with Gigina.

CHAPTER 8

Vale Aganor - Duruce

After the skirmish with the Tahnet sailors, I returned to the dark halls of the Aegis Monks instead of continuing to one of Vale Aganor's taverns or inns. I picked at a bland meal in our hall, then I wandered the musty corridors eventually peeking into one of the sparring arenas after the evening bells.

Staffs cracked as two of my fellow monks sparred in the sand. I was alone in their audience. They noticed my arrival, but ignored me as I leaned back against the stone wall to watch them.

Evenly matched, they danced in black robes around each other and parried with practiced moves. Were they secretly friends? Did that happen among the monks? I had tried to befriend one or two, but they had rebuked any continued camaraderie, even reminding me that we did not risk each other with friendship. I studied these two, but there were no smiles, just rote movements of their weapons.

Occasionally they attempted a surprise move, but few of the blows landed.

Had I come to this match out of loneliness, or a desire to burn off energy I couldn't shake? I didn't need another bruise. The taverns were still serving, and I could find sexual release with one of the late drinkers. Perhaps the guard whose name I couldn't remember would still be at the Copper Kettle. I shrugged to myself. What was I searching for? *Tea?*

"Ready for more?" Turben asked from the archway.

I jumped at his voice. *No.* "If needed." The more you resisted him, the worse the bruises. I could hope he was just testing my resolve. He did that on occasion.

Turben clapped and the two monks stopped. We met outside the ring, and they passed over their staffs. When they'd left, he faced me on the sand. "Three Tahnet pirates? You needed Nightarmor for that?"

I blocked the low strike and parried after a feint. "It seemed prudent." Had they been pirates?

Turben tried to catch my knuckles with a slide down my staff, but I spun the weapon and jabbed for his ribs. "Did you enjoy it? Armored against their swords?"

What had the guards said? I had enjoyed the challenge, until the end. When I didn't reply, Turben feigned a series of strikes before cracking into my thigh. I felt the welt rising as I jumped back and circled.

"You should have left it to the guards, but you wanted to jump in."

I couldn't argue the point, except there would have been two dead guards. The woman had been good. I wished I were sparring with her, but she'd be in the dungeons by now, awaiting the Queen's judgment.

I took the rest of the beating silently. Whereas Turben had worked my sides earlier; now my legs took the worst.

When he finally let me go, I made sure not to limp but strode resolutely to the rack to store our weapons. I had trained and sparred all my life, at least all of it that I remembered. It had saved my life numerous times, but today it just seemed like punishment.

Turben waited by the arch. "We'll start again in the morning."

I could hope for an assignment, something to take me away from Vale Aganor, or at least Turben. A mission came often without warning, at least to me. "Yes, my Shadow."

He headed into the hall without me. "No tea."

I paused and studied my pants. The bruises swelled underneath. I would go to sleep early. I would spar in the morning. However, I would have tea.

As I stepped into the hallway, I couldn't hear his footsteps ahead of me but caught his silhouette. I would pay dearly for disobeying him, but in the morning I would send word to Gigina.

Sleep came easy, but the dreams kept me from any rest. In the first, I befriended the strange, prophesying woman from the highlands, only to have Turben kill her. Each nightmare woke me, then I slept, and they would not end.

The next afternoon, I sat on the patio of Gigina's apartment, sipping tea from fine china. The musky black blend had bitter tones and a heady fragrance. It was not the best tea I'd ever tasted, but the thin, sweet biscuits were spiced in Tahnet style.

She wore a dark red dress with matching red gems in her coiffed white hair. As an ambassador, she had a palatial suite with a large antechamber that led to the patio. I couldn't be sure if the flowers I smelled were those in her many vases or from the garden three stories below. Inside the darker room, Gigina's server waited by a silver teapot and tray atop an ornate table with a lace runner.

Her attendant was a young woman barely in her teens. She was dressed in bright red livery that reminded me of the guards. The setting had been much like I'd expected, and a little too formal for me to feel at ease.

"These three Tahnet were evidently wanted by King Dior's constables. The woman is being held for them now." Gigina smiled as if pleased. Her excitement over yesterday's skirmish had dominated our conversation.

I couldn't be sure what we should be talking about. "What did they do?"

Her smile grew, thinning her lips. "They're pirates. Their ship had been sunk, stranding them on the beach, but they'd made their way here, to Vale Aganor. King Dior will be quite grateful."

The attendant flitted away at a quick knock on the apartment door. As Gigina craned to watch, I felt a relief that we might find something to change the subject. I shifted my bruised bottom on her hard seats. We would have been more comfortable sitting on her divans inside the suite.

Excited voices caused a commotion inside, and I placed her expensive cup on its saucer. I'd been afraid I'd break it since she offered it to me.

Gigina's cup drifted as she leaned to peer into the darker antechamber. "What is it?"

The young messenger puffed as he raced across the room. "Message, Madam. For the Queen's First." Sweat darkened the chest of his white tunic as he panted out words.

I pulled my hands back from the table and felt my pulse

quicken. Had Turben found out already? There were three flights of stairs up to Gigina's apartments if Turben had sent the boy. The Queen would have sent one of the Aegis monks from her floors above.

Our tea seemed over, and I had not gained any sense of friendship between Gigina and myself. The formality had been an obstacle, and my own whispering fears another. It had been ingrained into me that I risked anyone with my companionship. Every instructor and other monks had made it clear that part of my duty was to remain disconnected, even from them. I had hoped to betray that tradition, but this messenger had been sent to whisk me away.

Gigina snapped a curious glance at me before speaking sharply to the boy. "Out with it." Her saucer rattled as she placed her cup on it.

He still had not gotten his breath back so that his words came in short bursts between quick inhales. "Assassins are in the Temple of Gerais. They killed some Virgins and the guards who responded. They've got crossbows. Dressed all in black."

Not Turben. My heart began to race. The embroidered napkin dropped from my lap as I stood and peered over the balcony railing. The gold dome of the temple blotted out any view of the street in front of it. The peaceful white stone of the back side gave no indication of the violence which might be happening within. The surrounding gray-tiled roofs, buildings, and cobblestone were clear of any suspicious figures. There were no crowds or violence. At this height, the city murmured indistinctly.

"How many?" I asked.

The boy stuttered. "I don't know."

He spoke the truth, as he knew it. Nothing he'd said had triggered my truthsense.

Gigina snorted. "The guards should handle this."

I turned from view and studied the messenger. It would take a few minutes to race down the stairs and out into the city. *Too long.* Why did they need me? Even Gigina believed the guards should handle this, and Turben had just beaten that warning into my legs. Still, my pulse sped.

Her face formed a sour expression. "Who sent you?" she asked.

"A guard, Madam. The guards are stationed outside the temple. The assassins have crossbows, Madam." He sounded nervous, as if he'd made some mistake, but he told the truth.

My pulse steepened further, and my jaw tightened. *Scaling armor*, I thought to Khimmer.

Yes, Mistress.

I'd dressed in a long, pale blue tunic for tea, with full tights underneath. Nightarmor had been formed to filigreed rerebraces on my upper arms, delicate bangles and bracelets at my wrists, an ornate choker, a wide belt, and black boots with silver and gold scrollwork. These flowed into a light, agile armor with flexible shoes, almost slippers, and finger-less gloves except for thumb spikes; I had worn the same to kill Kloro.

Taking a sharp breath, I grabbed the railing. I needed to get to the assassins quickly, before they disappeared or harmed those outside the temple. "I'm going down," I said. The stairs would take too long.

I vaulted over the rail to the side, sliding my hands down the balustrades.

Gigina's voice pitched high. "Down the wall? Take the stairs, or better yet, send word for the guard to handle this."

I focused on the gray mortar between the castle's white stones. "I'm sorry about missing the tea. Can we try another time?" Turben would punish me for my breech of tradition, but I wouldn't give up.

"Damn the tea." Gigina scrambled to the side of the balcony. "You can't risk the Queen's First like this."

Gigina believed what she said was true, and it hurt in some way. Was that all I meant to her, the Queen's First? Not Ahnjii, but the bearer of the last Nightarmor, gifted with truthsense, and an assassin. Anger boiled up. I said nothing and dug a spike in to begin climbing down.

This is unnecessarily dangerous, Mistress, and you seem agitated.

Shut up, Khimmer.

Why had the guards not called for the Aegis monks in the monastery? The boy would not have needed to climb three sets of stairs, but descend one. Crawling down the side, I dug spikes into crevices that were too well mortared. *Damn me to Hades.* My right foot scraped free, threatening to let me plummet to the gardens below.

I lurched, caught a thumb spike against the top of stone, and swung over a second-floor balcony's railing. Dropping half my height, I didn't land inside, but slapped the rail to slow my fall and caught a balustrade with two hands.

I cursed the cowardly guards and the assassins inside the temple. My thighs scraped the wall, and I blamed Turben. The assassins would get no mercy when I arrived, and they were likely not wayward pirates.

Mistress, I must point out your disquiet.

Quiet!

Scrambling down stone designed to avoid scaling would of course be difficult. Being called away from a polite tea warranted being angry. Despite the light breeze, I felt hot inside Nightarmor from the exertion. An attack on the temple of Gerais made no sense. Every city had the same gods, though some were favored more than others.

At the bottom balcony, two winsome maids watched me descend past them. In another circumstance, I might have offered an inviting smile, but I was in a foul mood. Khimmer was right.

I slid purposefully to dig a toe into an arrow slit just over fragrant blooming camellias. Spinning, I dropped to the Queen's gardens of stone and brush. Nightarmor thickened into reinforced boots to cushion my landing.

The temple's dome rose high over the outer stone wall. I smelled only flowers. Excited voices cut through the wind. After all this, I hoped the assassins had waited for me. I'd managed to scale in a short time what would have taken much longer using the switchbacks of stairs.

Teeth clenched, I raced for the low outer wall of the garden and vaulted over. I hung from the top while Nightarmor thickened, then dropped twice my height to the path. I staggered, and every bruise complained.

Sword, helmet.

The back of a brick building had broken barrels piled against its walls. They should keep the area clear. Nightarmor flowed up, and my vision changed to Khimmer's, highlighting with orange and reds the people gathered to gawk in the street.

I dashed behind three buildings before I came to the manicured grass that surrounded the temple. Skidding around the corner, I had my sword in hand when I reached the cobblestone. I drew in deep breaths of sweat mixed with the musty tea. My heart pounded more than it should.

A guard lay outside with a crossbow bolt protruding from her chest. I recognized her and growled in anger. The people babbled but kept a good distance from the pillared entrance and steps.

Three red-uniformed guards had gathered but stood uselessly in a knot on the other side of the temple opening.

Crossbow bolts would not penetrate Nightarmor. I stomped up the stairs, though the guards wouldn't be able to see the scowl I burned at them.

In the short foyer, another guard had been taken down with a bolt to his neck. Blood had poured across pale marble until the pool reached the table to my left.

Virgins, naked women and men, lay dead inside as did another guard. Steps circled a dais topped with the statue of Gerais. Four red-orange figures hid in the drapes and behind statues that ringed the outer walls. The scent of blood added to the miasma inside my helmet.

I stepped through the guard's blood. "Come out and fight me." Muffled, I barely heard my own voice above the pounding of blood in my ears.

A man screamed and burst from his hiding place among the drapes. A Virgin, he raced toward me. Babbling about the assassins, he looked as though he might tackle me. My trained restraint buried in readiness, I resisted striking at him.

Mistress, I believe you are drugged. Your body temperature is elevated, and you are not reacting properly.

Shut up.

A bolt skimmed the bicep of the Virgin and clanged off my pauldron. Who did they fire at, me or the young man?

When he stumbled at my feet, screaming at the pain, I stepped around him toward the shape I believed had fired. Khimmer's vision had advantages and disadvantages.

Another bolt fired, and I centered on my target while I strode down steps and past fallen bodies. The assassin's aim was poor, and their shot glanced across the back of my vambrace.

A man's voice yelled from my left, and a second assassin wrapped in black slipped from the curtains with a bellowing roar. He held a sword above his head with two hands and ran with a blocky gait. *This is no assassin.* I wanted to kill him, nonetheless.

Mistress.

Blood boiling, I ignored Khimmer and slipped to the side when the man reached me. Another bolt twanged off my helmet. My slash cut the man's chest deep into the armpit while he slammed down his sword where I'd been walking.

I repositioned, expecting him to drop his weapon, but he hung on weakly with his left arm while lifting the sword high again. How this assassin had killed the guards, I didn't understand. This man had no training with a weapon.

I drove Nightarmor's blade into his heart.

Unskilled or not, I wanted both of them dead. I nearly shook from the pounding of my heart. The crossbow clattered to the floor, and a woman shrieked as she raced out of her hiding place behind a statue. She held a short blade straight out, her arm extended. I could have been naked and killed her considering her clumsy attempt.

Again, I stepped to the side at the last moment. A vicious swing neatly severed her head. I laughed while I did it.

Mistress, you must seek a healer.

Remove armor. I needed air.

Nightarmor melted off, leaving the sword in my hand and blood dripping off the tip. I stood panting over my carnage. The wrap that had hidden the woman's face was nearly cut off, but a black shard of fabric connected to her headless body. She'd been a middle-aged woman with black hair, brown skin, and a thin nose like my own.

My feet shifted as the last shape ran for the door; a Virgin screamed as she stumbled over bodies and steps. I held my place. My body screamed to chase after her.

Blood spray dotted the gray marble. I could have killed more, especially if there had been a true assassin among them. How had the guards not stopped these two?

I adjusted my footing as two red-uniformed guards burst in with halberds ready. My breathing remained a steady panting, but I managed a laughing snort. I wanted them to attack. I hadn't put away my sword.

Mistress.

They stood wary across the temple, a field of dead between us. The statue of Gerais peered down, emotionless.

Two more guards entered the temple escorting Gigina who paused, then carefully stepped over the body in the entry. "You're okay," she said, a note of worry in her tone.

I wanted to answer with a snide comment about the inexperienced attackers, but did little more than pant. Rage churned in my chest. My heart raced to the point it might burst. Perhaps Khimmer was right. I didn't feel right.

Yes, Mistress. You need a healer.

Perhaps.

Dress bunched in her fists to expose her ankles, Gigina circled the steps, careful to avoid stepping in blood, until she came within a few strides. Her eyes opened wide at the sight of the woman's head at my feet. I had not thought her squeamish. "Merciful Rhys." She peered from me to the woman, then to the man. Wizened hands dropped her dress and rose to press against her lips. Red jewels sparkled on her fingers. Her eyes were wide. "I know these people. They are not assassins."

Truth.

I trembled, suddenly angry at Gigina's antics. The couple dead on the floor wrapped in black were obviously not assassins. Why couldn't she just say who they were?

"Who?" I managed the word and searched for saliva in my dry mouth. "Who are they?"

The amount of dark red blood on gray marble dimmed the room. The guards stood close behind the pastel colored Gigina in what seemed a cowardly cluster. The threat was gone.

I glared at the woman's head on the floor with her face locked in a grimace of rage. She could have been an artisan or merchant that I'd seen on the streets of Vale Aganor.

Cautiously, Gigina reached for my face. I stiffened, but did not resist. Her cold fingers touched my hot skin and pulled my eyes up to hers. "Ahnjii, these are your parents."

Truth.

I blinked in shock. *Parents?* That wasn't possible. I was an orphan raised by the Aegis monks. Jerking away from Gigina's touch, I turned my attention to the head on the floor.

The killer had the same sharp, straight nose. How could it be? Gigina had spoken the truth, so how did she know? How had this been hidden from me? All my life I'd believed myself an orphan. I'd been left on the steps of the castle. Why had they lied?

The tip of my sword rose. I needed to strike something. My heart pounded in my chest.

Mistress, might I sheath your sword?

All this slaughter by my parents? Why? "How do you

know? How can these be my parents?" I could not take my eyes of the woman and couldn't call her mother.

Gigina's firm fingers returned to my chin, but I refused to shift my head. "I was there the night the Aegis monks brought you into the castle. They had kidnapped you."

Truth.

I stiffened, and my sword trembled with my racing pulse. The monks had stolen me, not rescued me.

Gigina continued, her fingers on my chin. "I was there the next morning when your parents petitioned the councilors to address the crime. They never knew it was the Aegis monks. In all this time, they believed you lost."

All truths.

The Aegis monks had lied to me as well, raising me as an abandoned orphan. They had shown me how to use my truthsense, my gift, the Touch of Nyx. *A curse.*

They had put the sword in my hand and taught me how to kill. They had lied to me, before I understood my gift, and I'd never questioned it. Turben left bruises on my body, but had stolen my life. I imagined thrusting Nightarmor's sword into his body.

Mistress—

Shut up.

I cannot, Mistress. Your emotions are altered. Your temperature and pulse are too high. You are in danger.

With my trembling left hand I absently touched my braid. Gigina studied me. She had known. Queen Meihlia had accepted my kidnapping along with the pledge of my life to her. She'd always seemed a just ruler; how could she allow this? Vale Aganor the benevolent kingdom was a lie.

They'd betrayed me and conspired to keep me from the family that I had just killed. The tip of Nightarmor's sword clattered on a step from my trembling. Had this been my family's vengeance? Why attack the Virgins of Gerais? Why not the Aegis monks?

Neither of my parents would have survived two steps into the monastery carrying a weapon. Even true assassins had never made it inside.

Mistress, something is wrong.

Yes, Khimmer, I have been betrayed.

Mistress?

I could enter the Aegis monastery and survive for a while. Perhaps long enough to exact some revenge. Nightarmor would protect me from their hidden crossbows and supply weapons once inside. They had caused me to murder my parents. I could make them regret that. I should feel remorse for the head at my feet, but anger pounded in my veins.

"Gigina, what was my name?"

"Ahnjii."

Truth. It was a common name.

I glared at the mother who named me while I trembled with rage. The first swift strike could be into Gigina for her betrayal all this time.

If it were not for her, I would never know. My mind had been dulled by emotions. Khimmer was right. However, I couldn't bring myself to sheath the sword.

Mistress, I believe you've been poisoned.

I'd been armored; nothing had pierced my skin or even touched it. I replayed the skirmish and gritted my teeth. They were never assassins, and I should have recognized that. They'd been fanatics. Their skills should not have been a match for the Queen's palace guards. Death filled the air with a stench inside the temple from their carnage.

"Why would my parents attack the Virgins?" I could make no sense of it. Why had the guards called me?

Gigina looked away, ignoring my question. Rage at her betrayal bubbled up. "Why?" I demanded. The guards shifted as I shouted.

She stepped back and shrugged as if to answer me.

Lie.

She did know why my parents had attacked the Virgins. What did she know about this? Was there more to the betrayal that hadn't been told?

I faced her, drawing my sword to the side. "Tell me what you know."

Her face blanched and she stepped closer to the guards. She shook her head, unwilling to answer me.

"What do you know about my parents' attack?"

She shook her head again, and her eyes widened.

Lie.

Gigina knew that I did not need a verbal response for truthsense. A disguise or a simple shrug would draw the attention of my gift.

I stepped forward and almost struck her. They had all deceived me my entire life. She tried to lie to me standing in the bloodied temple. Backing into the guards, she seemed ready to escape.

Mistress? Can you see how your emotions control you?

I blinked. Khimmer used the words Turben often said.

Did you know, Khimmer, of my parents?

I did not. I cannot hide my thoughts from you. I chose you and will serve until your mortal body dies. I believe you have been poisoned. Your emotions are wrong.

Even the guards stepped back toward the entrance.

I had not been cut, touched, or sprayed with liquid. Anything in the air would have affected the Virgins as well. How long had I felt this excitement or rage? Before I entered the temple. It had been there during the climb down the castle wall. Since I'd had tea on Gigina's balcony.

"Did you cause this? Did you poison me?" I shouted at Gigina. In a step I could reach her. The guards might intercede, but they hadn't even been a match for my parents, the false assassins.

Her shoulders sank as if in defeat. She looked down, and a grimace formed on her face. With a deep inhale, she stiffened and drew up straight. A wicked smile played across her lips. Gigina took a step toward me and spoke. "No." I smelled a mint tea on her breath.

Lie.

She wanted to die, burying her secrets with her. For a brief moment I shook, restraining myself. My jaw tightened, and I took a step back, lifted Nightarmor's sword over my back, and pressed it against the choker. It turned to liquid in my fingers as Khimmer absorbed it. I could feel their relief.

My body wanted to rage and move, but another part wanted to kneel beside my mother and cry. At the moment, I did neither. Steeling myself, I focused on my duty and obligations.

"Take her to the Queen for interrogation, by the order of the First Assassin."

Gigina shrieked, yanking a hairpin from her white hair. One of the guards caught her frail arm while a second stepped from the back to help restrain the ambassador.

I dropped to my knees in front of my mother's head. "Go, tell the Queen I will follow. Gain this traitor's confession." I rested my palms on my bruised thighs. My head still swam, but it would clear, and I would confront Turben, if not the Queen. "Send for a healer; I have been poisoned."

CHAPTER 9

I glanced up from petting the calico to find Vivianne studying me.

"If you're an orphan, why didn't the witches take you in as family?" Vivianne appeared perplexed.

The calico jumped into the seat it had occupied before I claimed Vivianne had big ears. The other cats had settled onto carpeted pedestals and counters, except for the gray tabby who wandered across the bookstore.

From the way Vivianne described witches, I wanted to meet one. "I guess there weren't many where I came from."

"Where's that?"

I blinked, not willing to tell her of Duruce, but not wanting to lie either. "Slovenia, before I came to Tallahassee." I hadn't even spent a full day there.

The gate home was there, and Tyler had promised to get us back so we could look for it. I had a duty to return home and would search for the way back properly.

However, the thugs would be after Tyler if we went to Slovenia, and I didn't want that. Somehow I needed to complete my duty and kill King Dior with Nyx's Blessed Blade without risking my new friends on Earth. I'd never been allowed friends, and might not return to them. I hadn't reconciled where I belonged yet.

Vivianne squinted at the high window above the bookcase. "Slovenia? Near Italy? I have family in Italy."

"Family, as in Fae?" I asked.

She straightened from where she leaned against the bookshelf and looked at the back employee door. She lowered her voice. "Yes." With a lithe step, Vivianne returned to the seat on the other side of the calico. "Best not to say that aloud, too often at least." She scratched along the cat's neck, making it purr. "You are very strange, Ahnjii. Others must have surely noticed. You should be careful not to get around the high Fae."

Tyler had warned the same about authorities from their governments. I'd tried to treat my time in Tallahassee as a covert mission.

"These high Fae, they're your leaders?"

Vivianne snorted. "No. Not that they don't act like it. They are pure Fae." Each time she named her people she lowered her voice. "There was a time, generations ago, when it is said that they were masters. They have skills we do not, such as sigil making, so they still have some power over us and others." She nodded toward me. "Witches have been known to trade service for service. Rather often."

I doubted I would be trading the use of my truthsense to anyone. "Pure Fae?"

Vivianne pursed her lips. "No, human ancestors."

I raised my eyes, appraising her thin form and gentle features. Sex with a Fae might be interesting, just to experiment. But I liked Vivianne, and wanted her as a friend. The monks had conditioned me to never have sex outside of release; otherwise, I could risk someone I cared for. Enemies might consider them worth threatening. They'd also prohibited all friendships, but I'd already broken that with Tyler.

She laughed. "What are you thinking about?"

My ears warmed as I looked at the cat. "I'd like to be your friend."

Vivianne laughed, almost a giggle. "Well, you are friendly."

It wasn't an answer, but it would have to do. It was as easy to talk with her as Tyler. Deanna often had agendas or advice. John would rather I had never existed, but he tolerated me for Deanna's sake.

After I'd spent most of the day with Vivianne, Tyler called. "Did you get lost?"

Behind me, Vivianne spoke to some new customers. I'd heard the speech so many times, I could have given it myself.

"I'm just hanging at the bookstore with a new friend," I said.

"Should I be jelly?" Tyler laughed. "Hungry yet?"

I was famished. Vivianne had already hinted that she'd be leaving soon, but I could come back anytime. "Pho?" I scratched a loving black cat along its cheeks.

"Okay. You're at the bookstore where Deanna left you?"

"Yep."

"Give me ten minutes." Tyler hung up.

Vivianne strolled behind the pair of women who called to the cats with voices pitched high like Deanna often did.

"Heading out?" Vivianne asked.

"Yes. Do you want to come with us? Pho."

She shook her head and spoke quietly. "Cars."

"I don't drive either, but Tyler does."

"Metal," she whispered.

I frowned, not understanding.

Vivianne laughed. "I'll explain later. You're an odd one, Ahnjii."

She meant it in an endearing way, but I knew that the oddness came from my newness to Earth. It had been awkward with Vivianne, more so than with Tyler, who had met me the day I arrived. I supposed I'd get better at faking everything and fitting in until I found a way home. Unfortunately, I had to keep Vivianne's secret from Tyler.

She let me give her a hug before I left, but she cringed, and I thought of Nightarmor's metal. Bounding down the steps, I skipped to Tyler's car.

"Who's your new friend?" they asked.

"Vivianne. She's great. The cats love her." I looked away, out the window, and tickled the bottom of my braid. It felt odd not telling Tyler that I'd solved the mystery of the people with tall ears. "I can visit anytime."

"Fabulous!" Tyler sounded genuinely happy. "Purely platonic, I'm assuming. This is good for you."

Platonic? I thought to Khimmer.

Nonsexual, Mistress. Though I derive that from an earlier obscure context combined with present reactions.

"Yes. A friend rather than just sex." We passed through College Town, and I watched the students gathering at the bars and restaurants. This section of town had little activity until the sun started to lower at the horizon. "Can I get a cat?" I asked. Deanna had Jake and Willie.

Tyler tilted their head and shook it. "I wouldn't push John that hard. He tolerates Deanna's tabbies."

"It's no more his property than mine."

"Deanna and John, they're a couple. She would agree

with him. Of the two of us, she's the oldest and most responsible, so she runs the house for our parents. If she hadn't come to Tallahassee for her psych degree, I probably wouldn't have picked FSU. We'd be in Manhattan." Tyler tapped the steering wheel with one finger as they drove. "You might eventually get your own place, nearby of course. Then you could get your own furry companions, but you have to take care of them."

John had suggested I find a place and a job. Did Tyler think I should as well? I couldn't stay on Earth forever, even though it was nice to have friends. My preference would be to live with Tyler and Deanna, even John, but I had a king to kill. Nyx would not forgive me if I didn't try to use her Blessed Blade and finish the assassination. Did she scorn me now?

"I need to go back to Slovenia and try to find the way home to Duruce."

Tyler nodded and shifted in their seat. "I know. I'll talk with Deanna again. She said she'd plan a trip. John has kept her busy with weekend plans. I'll talk with her."

"Thank you. I'm afraid that if I don't try, I'll never want to leave."

"Stay." Tyler responded quickly, almost urging me.

I liked that they wanted me here on Earth. "I have to finish this." Would I come back? The people of Vale Aganor had betrayed me, all of them. Besides, I had friends on Earth.

Tyler sighed, louder than usual. "Ok. If Deanna waits too long, we'll go ourselves."

I studied Tyler's face, and they had a tight, stressed jaw. "You can't go back there. Those bandits will still be looking for you. It's not safe for you." I didn't want them risking themselves.

"You've got to get home."

"I do." Deanna would have to agree to get me there. The vengeance over my parents mattered less as time passed, but it still hung there. King Dior had caused their death. "I have a mission to complete. A duty to fulfill."

CHAPTER 10

Vale Aganor - Duruce

I soaked at the end of the warm bath with my stomach still queasy even after a night's sleep. The splashing water from the clay pipe drowned any other sounds, not that the other monks spoke to me. Word had gotten out quickly, and though I should be the one with a grudge, they avoided interacting with me and barely offered a greeting unless they couldn't avoid it.

The fatty scent of lathered soap disgusted me, and my muscles hurt from retching up the healer's herbs overnight. The bruises from Turben's sparring had yellowed but still ached. My mood had quieted, though it had gotten no lighter when the poison's rage had been flushed from my system.

Turben had been right. He'd warned me not to go to tea. I'd wanted a friend and been betrayed.

They still questioned Gigina, and I might never know the results of the interrogation. I'd likely be sent off on another mission soon. Queen Meihlia tended to make good use of me, a tool formed by their own hands from the very beginning. How old had I been when they stole me, five or six?

I hadn't gone looking for Turben yet, but I would. He would answer my questions. Likely he'd be dispassionate and dismissive, but he owed me simple answers. I wasn't naïve. They'd used me, and I couldn't see another purpose in my life. I'd make him answer.

"My Shadow," Turben's voice called loudly from the side.

The other monks looked away from us. I hadn't noticed him walking in, though I should have.

"What do you want?" I had my braid in hand and flicked the soggy tip. Standing, I pointed at him. "Never mind. I don't care. I have some questions."

His expression remained unreadable. "I will answer them as we spar." He turned to leave before I could respond.

Scrambling, I exited the baths and made for my towel. I'd be happy to take a few swings at him, though I'd more likely end up bruised even worse than I was. Water soaked my tunic as I put it on over wet hair and my hastily dried body. The jog down the halls to reach the arena dulled my anticipation. I'd be lucky to get in a punch and would certainly leave with a new set of aches. This was my life.

Turben chose hand combat and grappled me into a throw before I could spit out my first question.

I rolled up to my feet. "Why take me from my parents?"

"I did not." He feigned a low kick and after a series of parries, caught me under the arm. "But it is common practice when we sense someone of your skill." He sprang at me, but I dodged a sweep at my knees. "You will be trained to search out children, when you are older."

I parried his kick, my jaw tensed, and I spoke through gritted teeth. "I will not." Did he think I would be responsible for orphaning a child?

Turben snorted. He rolled with a spray of sand at my face.

I took a solid kick to my unbruised side. Did he plan on covering me in yellow and purple? "Why not be honest with me? You could have told me my parents were alive."

"You would have approached them eventually." He drew me into overextending and struck my rib. "You would obsess. Act out. They would have been at risk. It was for their protection and yours."

"That didn't turn out well." Aching to strike him, I fell for a feigned parry, and he spun to punch the back of my shoulder, a sign of how badly I'd performed. I could hold my own with most of the monks, but Turben and a few of the other teachers were untouchable.

What questions did I really have? Why? That had been answered. I wanted some remorse on someone's part.

"None of this bothers you?"

"Death and shadows by the blessing of the Goddess."

I'd never hated that statement of faith before. Turben held no guilt for what he, or any Aegis, had done to my family. I'd expected he might turn this on Gigina, but he hadn't tried to avoid the blame.

I tumbled through sand from another blow and unclenched my fists. "Why should I remain?"

For the first time, emotion crossed Turben's expression as his eyes tightened. "Duty." He flew at me and finished our parry with a fingertip strike to the throat and a palm to my chest that threw me to the sand.

I coughed and regained my breath from the impact. He let me rise. My hands trembled as I pushed up. "Was it my duty to be taken from my family?"

"Yes." His footwork I parried, but he caught my side. I was equally bruised now.

Why couldn't I leave? I could move to the hot coast and load boats, learn to fish, or sell wares. Would the Aegis assassins kill me? If so, Khimmer would be released, and they could retrieve Nightarmor. Maybe I would have to go farther than the coast of Vale Aganor.

"What were their names, my parents? Do I have siblings? Other family?"

Turben struck without answering. I would never learn these things. Any family relations could be used against me.

I was being childish, but I threw up my hands and started walking for the side of the pit. "I'll have nothing to do with you. Any of you."

Turben sprinted ahead and pushed me back toward the center with two hands. "We are not done sparring."

I stepped around him. Would I try to leave? The Aegis monks would kill me. I had never heard of anyone ever leaving. Before, I'd believed they had unwavering faith in Nyx, Queen, and duty, but now I wondered.

Turben spun me from the shoulder and swept my knees, slamming me on my back. "Spar with me."

I glared at him as I rose. "No." Turning my back on him, I continued for the edge of the ring.

He came to my side this time, driving a knee into my stomach, then grasping my leg and neck to flip me. I nearly hit the stone that bordered the sand.

The air returned to my lungs in ragged gasps. Dots flicked across my vision. Turben crouched right above my head with no expression. I knew he was angry. So was I.

I desperately wanted to call out Nightarmor and grab Turben by the throat with a metal gauntlet. Instead, I yelled and lunged for his throat. A thoughtless move.

He caught my right wrist easily and twisted. Sand coated my lips and sweating forehead as he flipped me face down. Dragging me quickly, he deposited me in the center of the ring and dropped my hand before I could gain footing.

I leaped to my feet and during the rest of the sparring, I managed to land three glancing strikes. Turben carefully bruised my one side, upper arms, and shoulders before he let me leave.

We said nothing, and I didn't bother trying to lead the way or follow as he walked for the archway. Sweat and sand covered me, and I stunk. The toxins from Gigina's tea and the healer's herbs mingled with the sweat. I staggered down the shadowed halls trying to decide if I would head back to the baths or my bed.

Turben's silhouette disappeared in the darkness ahead. At the moment, I hated the man, but I often did. After the beating, I had no energy to feed my emotions or plan what I would do. I could tell from his reaction of anger that the Aegis monks would kill me if I tried to leave. What would I do anyway, pull fishnets? I had never enjoyed boats.

A shape moved ahead of me, and for a moment, I thought I'd caught up with Turben. The figure didn't move, though.

Whoever it was waited for me just before the next lantern with their face hidden in shadow. Had Turben told them of my threat to leave? Would they just kill me now and be done with it? Certainly they wouldn't give me time to raise Nightarmor. I doubted I could escape even then. They'd net me and drag me off to a cell to starve.

"What do you want?" My voice rasped and sand drifted off my nose.

Khimmer, if you hear a bolt fired, armor.

Yes, Mistress.

They waited until I took two more steps to answer. "The Queen calls."

My face tightened. She too had betrayed me. Would she have any regrets? Taking a deep breath, I responded. "I come."

I climbed the Queen's stairs to her apartments on the fourth level. Stinking and still dripping occasional sand, I stopped at the window overlooking Vale Aganor. The gentle murmur of the city barely reached these silent halls.

Last night, after I'd vomited the healer's herbs, detoxed with their tea, and soaked in the hot bath, the rage had drained from my body. As bitter as the tea, my mood had hung like a shroud. Sparring with Turben had only hardened my soul.

The city would never look the same to me. Market squares and trade shops spread to the farms and fields of the valley. These had always been under my protection. I was the Queen's dagger, and she safeguarded Vale Aganor. Using me, she didn't need troops draining the coffers or farmer's children to take up arms. They could grow up in their family homes, marry, and have their own children.

When I had no family, this had seemed a noble calling. Now I knew that my family had been the unwilling sacrifice, all because of my gift. If I had not had truthsense, I would have grown up with my mother and father. As what? I didn't even know if they were bakers or farmhands. I knew nothing about them. Did I want to? Would that just be more fodder for the bitter fire inside? Did I have siblings?

I patted down my braid and sand drifted under my

tunic. Nightarmor had formed ankle-high boots and its minimal form: a simple black choker with gold and silver filigree, a matching belt, and the bracelets and bangles on my arm. I wore my sweat-stained tunic to meet with the Queen.

The Aegis monk who had been sent to call me waited at the bottom of the stairs. I continued with dull footsteps across the broad landing with its elaborate windows, stopping at the last steps so I could glare up.

Aegis Monks stood every eighth step on each side of the broad steps. Black hooded robes hid their sex, and the guards wore gray masks to hide their faces. *Shapeless and uncaring.* I had learned the truth of them in one day.

Sharp incense drifted from the censers in the ceiling. Thirty-two steps led to the Queen's apartments. I let my boots echo slowly against the walls and my once fellow shadows. They were unmasked now as my abductors. I had been the final cut in my family's heart, but they had begun the thrust.

Hinges creaked above as the four monks at the Queen's audience chamber began opening the doors before I crested the flight of stairs.

I'd learned from Turben that none of the monks would regret what they had done to me or my family. Their hearts were cold. I'd been too young to know. Now, my only memory of my true family would be the image of their corpses, by my hand.

Queen Meihlia, draped in green robes and glittering gold and diamond tassels, rose from her throne. Uncharacteristically, she strode down the thin steps lined with golden statues of cephari. She had skin browner than my own and black wiry hair entwined with vines and flowers. Gold and blue shadows shined under her eyes while black dots had been painted in an intricate pattern over her eyebrows and down her cheeks.

The room stretched beyond with rows of yellow and green pillars. To my left, Gigina hung by her wrists, attached to manacles on the golden wall. Beside her stood a collection of councilors.

I dropped to a knee as the Queen approached. "My Queen." I had never seen her descend from her throne for any petitioner.

"My First, Ahnjii. You have my remorse for my deceit. I will not attempt to excuse my actions; they are those of a ruler." The Queen's tone firmed at the last sentence, then softened again. "However, I regret the pain it has caused you. I would not wish that upon you."

Truth.

I swayed, surprised at her near apology. Eyes locked on her sandaled feet, I stiffened.

Aegis monks lined the periphery of the room. I had no desire to forgive her or any of them. I had not expected her regret, however. "My Queen," I acknowledged.

"Rise," Queen Meihlia said, striding up steps to the wall where Gigina hung. "We have this traitor's confession for you to truthsense, and an assignment for you."

Those like myself who are touched by Nyx were rare. However, there were others, all within the Aegis monks. The truthsense made for excellent spies and assassins. Any of them could take the confession and verify it. Why wait for me? Any assignment would be a separate matter.

I followed, studying Gigina's face; her expression had dulled and broken from the fierce woman I had known. As expected, no torture showed on the ambassador's face or limbs. Her pale green, pleated robe still draped from her body. The dark manacles hung low enough that her heels remained firmly on the floor, but she sagged against the wall.

The Queen walked up the dull, gray stone that led through the columns to the outer edge of the chamber. White and blue frescoes decorated the ceiling. Each of the gods' insignias were carved into the floor. A scribe, his robes white with silver thread woven in the hem, waited with pen and ink at a podium that had been brought in.

Gigina smelled of sweat even over the incense. I imagined it could be me as well.

The Queen stopped a few paces away and raised her hand to my shoulder in a familiar, almost maternal pose. She had no right.

A red-faced councilor scurried to meet us. "My Queen."

She only nodded to him. "You may begin your confession."

Coughing and intertwining his pudgy fingers, he turned to Gigina. "Speak."

The ambassador's eyes appeared not to recognize any of us, but the purple ring of Phantasos hung at the outer edge of her irises. She never focused on me at all.

"I have acted under the orders of my liege, King Dior of Tahnet." Grating, Gigina's voice held no strength. "I poisoned the parents of the Queen's First Assassin so that they would wake enraged in the Temple of Gerais. The guards Ilianos, Aen, Makiba, and Yarin aided in their capture and placement in the temple. The merchant Jynisvet smuggled the vials in for me.

"I drugged the Queen's First Assassin so that she would kill them. Cyn, the captain of the guard, made sure that she was called to the temple. After she killed her parents, I broke to her the secret of her history, so that she would seek vengeance upon the Aegis Monks.

"I planned that she'd be unable to resist attacking them, and thus disgrace her, solely to remove her from service. Once I had completed my mission, I was to contact King Dior so he could activate an assassin against the Queen's consort, Stehl."

Truths.

"All truths," I said. My mouth felt dry. The stench of Gigina's and my own sweat made my stomach churn.

Queen Meihlia's voice came crisply, speaking directly to the councilor. "Why did King Dior wish Stehl killed?"

The scribe scratched across his paper, and the councilor repeated the question.

Gigina coughed thick with sputum. "King Dior wished to disrupt the commerce in the Phalyn Basin. Stehl is prominent there."

Truth.

I blinked. My parents had been killed over coins and taxes. They had been targeted, just to manipulate me. I had gone from being an orphan without any history to being an orphan with a twisted, sordid past. All to gild a king's house.

The scribe coughed.

"Truth," I whispered.

Queen Meihlia turned me toward her. "You will approach Nyx and supplicate for King Dior's death."

I clenched my fists so they would not shake. This was why I had been their truthsense today.

"Yes, my Queen." With my parents' blood fresh on my hands, the Queen manipulated me. She used Gigina's deviant plot to enhance the supplication. I would, too. Gigina would be dead, but King Dior's blood could be mine. Only Nyx could bless the killing of a king. I could not have revenge upon the Aegis Monks for their part, nor the Queen's, but my cause might convince Nyx to allow the King's death.

Whatever came of this, nothing would wash the blood from my hands or theirs. My oaths were a thin veil to hide my pain and no longer the heavy cloak of loyalty. I had lost so much in one day. I grieved for the lie I had once believed.

I reached the threshold and almost forgot myself. Turning to face her with a steady expression, I knelt.

The Queen had returned to her throne and studied me even as she nodded for me to leave.

The shapeless faces of the Aegis Monks watched as I raced down the broad steps and whipped past the windows. Outside lay the city that had orphaned me.

On the landing of the second floor, I took a breath, slowed, and walked with a shuffle that echoed Nightarmor's metal boots across marble walls.

Turben had refused to tell me who my parents were. Gigina had never named them. I was no less alone than I had ever been. I'd never been close to the Aegis monks who had abducted and lied to me. The only person I considered befriending had betrayed me.

I didn't know what life lay ahead of me, but I would kill King Dior, Blessed Blade or not. I ached, but still sped my pace to the Aegis monastery where the temple of Nyx awaited me.

CHAPTER 11

Vale Aganor - Duruce

The heavy wooden door to the Aegis monastery closed behind me with an ominous thud. I stepped down the dark stairs with dull metal footsteps echoing off stone walls.

Shadows played along the walls, and the air turned musty. The last remnants of sand flew out as I flicked the end of my braid.

I'd supplicated Nyx for a Blessed Blade three times before, the first with Turben present. Committed to a mission, I would not have to answer any call to spar. This would be my second time killing a ruler; the first had been Queen Pertikka of the Arris Isles. Her ships had blockaded any who would trade with northern shores, including Vale Aganor.

I turned in the direction that would lead past the arenas, the kitchens, and the refectories. No monks showed themselves, but I could hear distant activity. Did they know of

Gigina's plans? She had tried to aim me at them like a weapon.

The last corridor would lead me deep under Mount Ergus. A natural tunnel said to have been carved by the Goddess herself, it had three elaborate sigils carved in the rock above the entrance. A brazier stood by the entrance, and ready torches waited in a wire repository on the opposite side.

I took the rough wood in my hand and dipped its sodden tip to the flame. With a dull whoosh, the torch added light to Nyx's temple entrance.

Three steps inside, the air grew humid and thick. The floor had irregular shapes and holes, forcing me to place each step carefully. The decline bore toward an unnatural blackness that swallowed my torchlight. The only sound was my own footsteps.

I cringed as an image of my mother's head flashed in my thoughts. What had she been like? Pleasant and cheerful despite losing me? Had she still wondered where I'd been taken? Her expression had been a grimace of pain and rage.

Gigina had caused my mother's death; I'd been the weapon. My foolish desire to have friends had been used against me. Turben had been right.

Still, I longed for that camaraderie that I'd witnessed with the Silari. Would I be able to finish this mission and never return?

The Aegis monks would hunt me down. Their spies were everywhere.

Ahead, a single drip sounded in a distant pool of water. It echoed down the tunnel, almost in time to my footsteps. The temple of Nyx was close.

My torchlight lit the carvings that began on the walls,

ceiling, and floor. Seemingly random, they became more frequent with each step and seemed to move in the flickering light. The tunnel ended in a circle of pitch black, the drip louder than my footfall, and the opening fully inscribed with carved sigils.

I took a deep breath and could taste the mold and rot in the wet air. My own stench provided nothing more than a sharp note.

My first step disappeared through a cloudy murk before splashing into black liquid. The torchlight didn't touch any walls or ceiling. Sluggish ripples reflected a few steps in and then disappeared. Still, I slid my torch in the sconce beside the opening.

The liquid sloshed into the top of Nightarmor's boots as I knelt. My braid slapped against the surface as I placed my forearms to the rock below and submerged my face with my eyes open. *Cleanse me.* Black and thick as blood, I could see nothing.

I stood and the thick liquid dripped off, returning to the pool, except the residue trapped in my boots. As I stepped forward, I could feel liquid slosh inside and around Nightarmor, no deeper than my ankle. *Tongue and blade sheathed, I come in petition.*

The torchlight reached the black altar ahead. Rough-hewn, smooth stone made up the waist-high table, a single block that rose from the floor.

Goddess, I beseech thee.

The air seemed to thicken as I approached. The blackness drank any torchlight that passed the altar. I placed my palms on the cold stone. *I claim King Dior for his crimes against mine, my Queen, and my country.*

I felt chilled to the bone, as if the temperature had

dropped in her temple. The black statue behind gained form, or the air thinned between us. Her features were hardened beauty, and black hair blended with draping robes. A cowl loomed over her head. I turned up, leaving my hands on the altar.

I had visited the dark side once and witnessed the stars. Deep in the ceiling above, lights twinkled above the statue of the Goddess, much as the night sky, except the darkness reigned here.

The lights dwindled as a dark fog descended. In moments, it poured onto the altar and obscured my hands. They roiled there, fashioning a hidden shape that I knew Nyx created.

She had accepted my plea. A Blessed Blade forged upon the stone. I resisted a shiver. This weapon pierced all, including Nightarmor.

I would avoid the trade routes where King Dior would expect me. Once word reached him that his treasonous Gigina had been taken, he would prepare for me. Arrogant, he would have his own Aegis monks searching for me. His assassins might still be sent for the Queen's consort.

He would not assume that I would cross the Minaoan waste.

The Blessed Blade glowed a deep red, like magma through rock. As it had the previous times, the thick fog lifted from the altar slowly as if it were rising steam. I couldn't see the statue of Nyx for the density of the cloud. The Blessed Blade lay finished on the altar.

Thigh sheath, I thought to Khimmer.

Yes, Mistress.

Nightarmor trickled down my hip and formed a band and sheath high on my outer thigh.

Ahnjii. The thought came to my mind much as Khimmer did, but where Khimmer had no sex, I knew this to be female. Nyx herself was speaking to me. *I would know your path.*

The fog paused in its ascent and flowed around my face. The distant drip faded to the hum of my blood inside my ears. I could see only black, though my eyes opened wide. Alarmed, I inhaled a heavy cloud of the thick wet blackness.

A sound came to my mind of distant tinkling, as if it rained broken crystal somewhere. A light moved in my vision, a fire down below amid a swarming mass. I watched from a rampart.

I spun to search Nyx's cavern. Acrid smoke vented in through Nightarmor's helmet. The Queen's guard and Aegis monks crouched beside me on the hazy ramparts.

Crossbows twanged and thudded in their hands. I stood ready for battle, a defender of the walls.

I had not called for armor, and I was no longer in Nyx's temple.

Khimmer, where are we?

For the first time that I could remember, Khimmer was not with me. A cold panic crept across my arms. When my skin touched Nightarmor, I felt trapped.

Khimmer!

Those about me fought a battle from the high reaches of the Queen's castle. The dark mass below, nearly hidden by the smoke, was Vale Aganor. Fires lit the city to my left side. The temple and spires of Rhys were gone. Flames licked from what should have been rooftops.

At this height, I could hardly hear distinct sounds in the din below, but a single scream pierced the smoke and my heart. A child's voice wailed.

There was war in Vale Aganor. It couldn't be possible, but it spread before me. At the base of the castle, hasty barricades blocked the stairs. I could make out the black robed Aegis monks, red-uniformed guards, and a motley mix of others defending it.

The attackers wore shiny black armor. Their helmets were smooth with protrusions that could have been pincers on an insect. Their weapons flared, and defenders died.

No matter how I got here, or where Khimmer had gone, I could not stand here atop the fortifications.

As I pulled back to search for the stairs down, I found my sword in hand. Had that been there the entire time?

Khimmer?

I was still alone. The realization gripped my heart.

Shaking away the fear isolation brought, I worked around those firing crossbows toward an opening where a young servant girl brought a basket of bolts.

She peered in terror over the edge as she refilled their quivers.

The stairs down through the walls were dark and opened into a section just below the steps leading up to the Queen's apartments.

People shouted orders from downstairs, and I clattered toward them. On the next floor, townspeople were piled up against walls, and an Aegis healer worked on their wounds. She had her hood back and worked a splint on a large man's leg.

"Who is attacking?" I asked.

She didn't respond, her attention on her ministrations. The man stared up at the ceiling.

"Is it Tahnet?"

She ignored me. Did the Aegis monks still shun me?

I jolted toward the next set of stairs. "Damn me to Hades."

The lower floor had those who were more severely wounded and a stack of bodies that I could only hope were dead. Mangled and bleeding on each other, they left a puddle that spread along the grout lines. The scent of death hung in the room, and the whimpers of the dying competed with the shouts for bindings and supplies.

Children scurried between healers, and guards carried the wounded. Explosions, fireworks or such, blasted from outside when the guards let in one of their own who was bleeding from his side.

I ran for the open door. "Who is it? Tahnet?" I shoved through when they nearly closed the door upon me.

The mayhem and uproar outside surpassed anything I'd ever seen or heard. The smoke clung thickly and rolled across the ground. It reminded me of my last moment in Nyx's temple.

Halberds rang on dull sounding metal, and the invaders' weapons blasted flame and metal. I had arrived too late. The strange figures walked with slow determination and had almost reached the barricades.

Townspeople beat on them with artisan hammers and died as well. In the moments it took me to race down the steps, not one of the invaders fell.

I wove through the clumsy metal and wood the guards had fabricated and leaped over fallen bodies. Aegis monks fought with pike and staff, but they too fell in the face of the weapons.

I rained blows on one of the invaders, striking joints and finally their hand and the weapon itself. Nightarmor's blade scraped and rang, but found no opening. Smoke burned my eyes.

Khimmer, close vents.

My heart dropped as I realized I would get no response.

The attacker's black helmet appeared one piece, with a thin line connecting it to the smooth gorget. I jabbed Nightarmor's tip into the crevice, but it slid past.

Their weapon exploded, pressed against my chest. Nightarmor vibrated and metal shrieked.

I staggered back. Pain welled from my back. A hole, the size of three fingers, puckered into my armor. I coughed wetly. My legs wobbled and gave way while my sword rattled to the slick cobblestones.

The invader stepped over me. Vale Aganor would be lost.

I inhaled sharply as the black fog released my head. My boots sloshed as I staggered back from Nyx's altar.

I coughed. "What was that?"

Only the steady drip of water answered me. *Tongue and blade sheathed,* I thought to myself.

I bowed my head to Nyx. *Tongue and blade sheathed, I come in petition. What happened to me? Is Vale Aganor under attack?* I asked Nyx.

The fog had lifted, and light twinkled in the distant ceiling of the temple.

I could not help myself. *Khimmer?*

Yes, Mistress. You've asked me never to interrupt you in this temple.

I had made them promise, but smiled and sighed with comfort that they were with me. It had been a vision of sorts. A horrifying warning of war, perhaps.

Nothing. Shh.

I would have to tell the Queen before I left. The exit from the monastery, the primary one, came up near the main castle doors. I would know soon enough if this was a sight into the future or present.

Interrupted by Nyx, I approached the altar again where the Blessed Blade waited with an inscribed black handle and black obsidian for a blade. It could only be used for the victim of the supplication; any other use would bring the wrath of Nyx upon those who wielded it.

I picked up the blade with my right hand and cut a thin trace in my left palm, leaving drops of blood on the altar in return for the gift. Thinking of my mother, I relished the pain.

I held the blade and felt no excitement or even need for vengeance. Even with Khimmer returned, I felt lonely.

With a quick move, I sheathed the weapon and backed carefully from the altar. I had never heard of Nyx offering visions. Some of the other goddesses and gods were purported to do so.

Backing to the entrance to the temple, I lost all sight of Nyx's altar and statue. I repeated the obeisance, feeling all of Turben's bruises. Thick liquid dripped off my chin as I reached for the sconce. The rough wood of the torch was warm and real in my palm.

I jogged across the jagged natural floor out of Nyx's temple. Part of me knew that no attack raged in the city above, but I needed to check. Then I would approach the Queen again and beg an audience to tell her of this.

I smiled, knowing Turben would be upset hearing about it after I'd left. On a different day, I might have sought him out first. If I hadn't just learned that everyone I knew had betrayed me and my parents, abducted me, and lied to me, I might have been in a more gracious mood.

What did this vision mean for our future? Was this what would befall if I did not succeed in my mission?

Determined, I dropped the torch in the bin beside the brazier outside the temple and ran for the stairs.

I would cross the Minaoan Waste, kill King Dior, and return to Vale Aganor. Then I would see where the future would lead me.

CHAPTER 12

Minoan Waste - Duruce

In the guise of a minstrel, I marched dutifully through the streets of Vale Aganor. The evening bells were ringing from various temples, and some shops were already closed while other owners chatted with lingering clients. The aroma of family dinners drifted from chimneys. Children laughed and scurried for their mealtimes. In a short while, the streets would empty, and families would settle in for sleep.

I took the same path out of the city that I had just walked from my last mission. In this case, I would cut through the mountain range that ended at Mount Ergus and skirt the dry crags and ravines that led to the Minaoan Waste.

There were very few who lived in the dry desolate rocks, and King Dior would not expect me to take the extra time to reach him. I could be patient. I had no great hurry to return when my mission was complete.

Turben would be furious that I'd left without reporting

to him, especially after my second visit to the Queen. She'd listened carefully, and scribes had taken my words. If the vision had not come from Nyx, we all would have marked it as a nightmare. I'd left Turben a message with one of the monks.

Khimmer had been concerned over my mood as I sped out of the castle. They were quiet as I relaxed, nearly out of the city. Three children shouted over a game of hoop in front of their dark pink and red house. Around the corner lay the road darkward.

The mountains rose at the horizon where their high peaks protected Vale Aganor from the worst of the darkside weather. Farms and pastures lined the road leading out of the city. Dressed in a brown merchant's apron, Turben leaned against a fence, waiting for me.

"Hades take me," I muttered under my breath. He couldn't stop me now that I was on a mission.

Moving casually, though his eyes flicked at children, houses, and myself, he straightened and began to walk in the same direction. I quickened my strides to pass him. With longer legs, he easily kept up.

"Tell me of this vision," he said.

I quickly retold my tale in a clipped, factual form with barely a breath. Expediting the information might lessen the time I had to spend with Turben. Despite my hopes, he required clarification on several elements, and his escort lasted until we passed the farms and walked the narrower trail darkward.

Turben finally seemed satisfied. "King Dior will expect you."

I had no requirement to discuss my plans with him, but I did. "I'll be coming through the Minaoan Waste. He will expect me to come along the coast."

"Perhaps. He is no fool, and his life depends on killing you." Turben spoke with a quiet reservation.

After I strode without a response, Turben spoke sharply. "Your path is your own."

I bristled at the comment. If anything had been made clear from Gigina's treachery, I had little choice in what my life had become. "I have nothing of my own."

Turben stopped, finally letting me continue alone. "Night's blessing."

I never turned back to watch him. My chest hollowed into an empty shell, and I focused on my steps. It wasn't until the next morning that I diverted from the road and disappeared into the thick forest that cloaked the foothills.

Four days later, I crested a ridge of green hills beyond the Saihin white waters. The early morning air smelled fragrant with delicate jasmine blooms and wolfsbane with its damp, woodsy scent. The wind that blew from the north carried bitter, dry air. The wasteland ahead formed a flat horizon, no more than a gray line.

The distant rapids roared in contrast to the silence of the tortured desert. I belonged there with the emptiness and silence. The ruins of the city of Bora melted into the slope of the foothills with vague shapes of buildings that had at one time been turned liquid, dried, and now weathered the effect of harsh wind and dust. Had the ageless Queen Meihlia known this city in its prime?

The surreal forms had always appeared chilling and distorted. I felt a kinship with them now. My soul empty, I was little more than a husk.

Cloak, I thought to Khimmer.

Yes, Mistress.

Nightarmor draped down to my feet and adjusted to a lightly armored mimicry of the stone upon which I stood. In this state Nightarmor would act solely as camouflage. For a short time, I could blend in and become nothing.

The desert stretched to the sunward horizon in a deception of its own. It would take a day and night to cross it. The dunes rose and shifted, some pure gray dust, others black, war-baked stone. My water bag slung full across my shoulder under the adapting cloak. Nyx's blade felt cold in its sheath on my thigh. Fine sand threatened to plume under my steps, forcing a slow pace.

I couldn't place my feelings over my parents properly. Never having known them, I found it hypocritical and dramatic to miss them. I grieved at the loss; that seemed proper. What the Aegis Monks and Queen Meihlia had taken from me couldn't be returned. Aegis training left me with the acknowledgment of a cold hard distrust for those I had relied on. The Queen had been sovereign over Vale Aganor for forgotten generations, and the selection of those with truthsense for an early indoctrination probably constituted a normal practice for the Aegis Monks. I couldn't fault the logic, but it made the betrayal no more palatable.

I navigated around a black pit where the rim had melted to glass. The distant sun never shone upon the bottom. As I passed, I searched the shadowy depths for any threats. There would be none in a land the goddesses and gods had forsaken.

Mistress? You seem distracted, Khimmer thought.

I am distracted. After all that has happened — of course I am. I crested a ridge and scanned the waste. Nothing moved, but I was less alert than my mission called for. The air smelled of sunbaked sand and dust.

Ambassador Gigina had been your friend.

Heat rose on my cheeks. Gigina had been my mentor on state politics, no more. I had no true friends, and no one that I could trust. *She was no friend,* I thought. Khimmer could not understand my emotions, but they did attempt to interpret.

My apologies, Mistress.

Frustrated, I strode over the ridge as it led into a shallow wave. Hard rock rolled smooth as if the stone had rippled, then froze into shape.

Nightarmor flowed up my neck mid-stride. *Mistress!*

I crouched at the alarm too late. A crossbow slid off the back of my arm and pierced my Nightarmor before it had fully formed across my back. As the metal hardened, the shaft splintered, leaving the remnant in my back. My vision shifted to Khimmer's as they poured a helmet over my head. I could smell my blood. Metal tainted my tongue.

Poison, Mistress.

Hades. I'd been an idiot. *Sword.* Sliding down the rock slope, metal screeched against rock. Khimmer formed my hilt at my left shoulder.

An assassin wrapped in gray and black rose ten paces away. They discarded their crossbow and drew a blade from their waist. They should have run. Nightarmor at its full measure could not be pierced by an ordinary blade.

Digging heels into the slope, I jerked upright. My back twinged. I could feel a sluggishness to my muscles. Whatever toxin they'd used, it hadn't paralyzed me. I pulled my sword and positioned my left side toward them.

Two more assassins approached, their shapes orange in Khimmer's vision. One came from behind, and the second from the right, running down the gullies in the stone waves.

I ignored them for the moment. Leaping, I slashed at the assassin who had shot me. They deflected artfully and rolled to the side. My next strike caught their arm and I spun, dragging the tip to the back of their shoulder. Flesh and leather split open, raw and red. I landed crouched behind the first assassin so all three were in front of me.

One wielded a Blessed Blade. King Dior had placed a contract on me. That edge could pierce Nightarmor. My heart raced, either from the battle or the poison.

Mistress?

I'm fine. No wonder the first assassin had pressed.

I focused on the bearer of the Blessed Blade. Jumping across two ripples, I put them closer and led with my sword. My blade, part of Khimmer themselves, could be damaged by Nyx's weapon as well.

Spines.

Yes, Mistress.

Hand-length spikes grew from my pauldrons, couter, and vambrace. They could be cut but could help me avoid a direct strike. My left arm felt cooler, even numb. I needed to end this before the poison deteriorated my responses any further.

The blade bearer, a woman from her shape and movements, circled a bubble of molten stone. I sprinted and struck low. I slashed at her left foot and exposed my right shoulder.

She didn't take the easy strike. Instead, she danced uphill and crouched. Perhaps she was waiting for her partner or the poison.

I gave her another target. Slashing a wide miss across her face, I pushed forward, exposing my chest.

She took it. Lunging, she stabbed toward Nightarmor's gold and silver filigree.

I tilted my left shoulder inward while continuing my swing. My spikes almost trapped the woman's wrist, but she was quick. Flipping my sword against my back, I spun. I risked exposing my back, but calculated she wouldn't have the leverage to penetrate Nightarmor.

Mistress?

I knew my thinking had fogged from the toxin, but I'd committed.

The Blessed Blade scratched against sword and armor, but it had no force.

I finished my turn, whipping up my sword. The blade caught her forearm mid-jump. Glancing off her leather and mail vambrace, I still had the momentum and position to finish the stroke under her chin.

The Blessed Blade vanished into smoke as the woman fell. How had King Dior known to intercept me here, in the Minaoan Waste?

Too sluggish, I turned to find the third assassin slamming into me. Together we rolled downhill. I could feel a spike on my forearm press and then pierce his chest. The leg I threw out to brace myself buckled.

We rose instead of stopping, tottered together for an agonizing moment, then smashed down onto a black bubble in the rocks. Like grating glass, it shattered.

Mistress!

I sucked in a breath, but in the confines of Nightarmor's helmet I got little air. We dropped. Khimmer adjusted, thickening. The inside of the armor pushed away, braces forming to cushion for impact. Blackness swallowed me, and I couldn't be sure it wasn't the poison.

I hit chin first, just over the assassin's shoulder. Lights flashed in my vision. I felt my water bag burst.

Mistress?

Khimmer adjusted my vision for the darkness. The assassin showed dark red but unmoving. Vague shapes formed for the walls of the cavern. I'd been sloppy and distracted. How far had I fallen? Blood trickled down my back. I couldn't feel the remnants of the shaft; too much of my body was numb.

Dizzy. Poison or impact? The hole above was a circle of light. I considered rolling over.

Mistress? You must get up. Search for a way to climb out.

I'm getting up. I stared at the glinting blade and the still warm assassin. Nightarmor contracted across my chest, applying pressure to the wound. My eyes bulged. My ribs might have been bruised.

You are not getting up. Your heartbeat is slowing.

I forced a knee to scrape across stone. With my right palm pressing down, I got both knees under me. The light looked too high for me to reach. Little of it played on the walls leading to me.

I'm up. Agile, helmet. I still wanted Khimmer's vision.

Yes, Mistress.

Nightarmor thinned, retracting so that aching joints moved easier and cool air seeped around my mouth and neck. Blinking, I searched the walls up to the hole above. It seemed as if I were inside a dome shape without scalable walls. I reached my sword and placed it on my back for Khimmer. They absorbed it with little more than a ripple at my neck.

I stood, shakily. The poison had worked into my muscles, and they moved with slow deliberation. Turning, I found an odd shape through Khimmer's vision.

A door, Mistress?

Shapes curved and straightened. *A gate?* Ends formed smaller circles as if embellishment, and some tapered into sharp points, as if to ward off trespassers from climbing through. I stepped closer. The arch above had unreadable markings.

I forced my right arm up and a foot forward. The toxins had me swaying. I couldn't piece together the shape. The gate appeared to have no walls. Some useless ruin. I nearly fell. *Hades.* I would die down here.

More to lean than to open it, I placed my hand on the gate. My fingers passed through, never touching metal.

Mistress!

Gravity shifted, and I fell headfirst into a dark room of dull gray sunlight. I found the floor had somehow moved to my side and slammed down onto it. Lanterns burned golden overhead. None of this made any sense. The world spun. Above, gray clouds covered the sky. Cool air flowed off a tile floor. I couldn't understand how this existed deep under the Minaoan Waste. It couldn't. I turned my head, and my stomach twisted into knots. I'd survived the assassins, if the poison didn't finish me. I wretched acrid bile as Nightarmor opened to fresher air. Perhaps I hadn't persevered.

Mistress?

The lanterns danced with the gray sky before everything faded to darkness.

CHAPTER 13

Tallahassee - Earth

I followed Tyler into the Ramnath family home and drew in familiar scents of potpourri, cats, and past meals. I'd lived here for months. With Tyler's help, I'd learned English and how to read it. We'd eaten meals together and weathered John's grumpy intolerance of my presence.

Jake and Willie watched us from a sunlit window.

"Deanna?" Tyler called out.

"Kitchen," she responded.

My chest had grown tight, fighting against duty and my own desires. We'd procrastinated long enough. We found Deanna scrubbing a clay pot in the sink.

"What's up?" she asked.

Tyler slid into a chair at the counter. "We need to discuss Slovenia."

Her shiny, black hair had been swaying with her the movement of her task. It paused. Then she resumed her scrubbing. "Okay." Normally she had much more to say.

"I'm healed," I said. "I have to try and go home. The last time I asked, you said you had a conference and we would speak afterward. That was a long time ago."

Deanna didn't turn. "You said you weren't sure where it was, this place."

Tyler and I had spent weeks going over photographs on their computer, and we'd picked out the turn where John had hit me with the van. A long ridge promised to be where the gate back to Duruce was located. Khimmer and I had both been disoriented, so neither of us could determine how long I'd fallen or walked to get there.

Tyler rolled an orange in the bowl on the counter. "We have a general idea. I could bring a drone and search before we climb. The backside slope is much easier."

"You can't go," Deanna said. "They don't have your name, but they know what you look like. I won't take the chance. I can take Ahnjii, if she really has to go."

We'd had the same conversation, or close to it, the last time.

"I have to go." King Dior had to die. I'd had to force myself into remembering my duty, and that in itself brought some guilt. I'd hidden Nyx's blade under the floor of the skating rink, and it should never be used on anything but the intended target. "I have to."

Deanna turned off the water and turned to study me, then Tyler. "Tyler, you can't go. I can find an investigator to search as you suggest." She shivered. "Don't put me through that worry again."

Tyler picked at the rough skin of the orange with one nail. "Okay."

She flicked something off her blouse and stared at me. "I've grown to like you here, but I can understand your need to finish whatever happened in Slovenia. I won't lie and tell you I believe everything you say about some other world." If she believed any part of my story, it was Nightarmor, which she had seen and never mentioned, and my truthsense.

"But you'll try," Tyler said.

Deanna took a deep breath as she nodded. "Yes. I'll get some recommendations for an investigator, pick one, and even ask them to do some preliminary scouting. We'll set a date to travel. I need to go through my schedule. How many days?"

My chest had emptied with her words. I didn't want to leave. Part of me imagined sneaking back to Earth after killing King Dior, but I wouldn't, not without the Queen's blessing. "Three or four?"

A nervous smile dashed on and off her face. Deanna scratched at her neck and straightened. "I'll get on it." She headed for the stairs.

"Thank you," I said.

Tyler hadn't looked up from the orange they were tormenting. "Are you sure?"

"That I have to go?"

"That you want to go."

I didn't, and that made it worse. "I have a duty."

"To kill someone."

My back stiffened, and I crossed the room to stand at the counter. "I'm not a soldier. I kill so that Vale Aganor never has to go to war."

Tyler tossed the orange back into the bowl. "Sorry. I've just grown used to having you here." They turned their face up and smiled. "Want to skate?"

I thought of the Blessed Blade under the building, but returned the smile. "Love to."

CHAPTER 14

Unknown location

Mistress?

The air smelled foul, ripe with my retching. The only sounds in the silence were my heartbeats.

A wheel hung over me. Its sides nearly touched the arches of the round cage. The lanterns hung from chains at the spokes. I still saw their steady flicker through Khimmer's vision. There was no ceiling or cavern above, just sky, which roiled with thick, gray clouds that seemed too close. Light leaked through gaps as if a sun lay impossibly overhead.

Remove helmet. I felt sick, dizzy. It didn't account for where I was, but I could barely think.

Yes, Mistress.

Cool air rushed in around my cheeks. Six metal gates in six stone arches circled us. Gray fog ebbed outside the bars. Pushing up on dusty tile with a shaky elbow, I asked, *Where are we?*

Khimmer hesitated. *I don't know. I'm not connected*

here. It is disturbing, Mistress. There had never been a time when they'd used that term. I almost sensed distress from them.

Beyond the gates a small platform circled the cage. Each gate looked identical. Through the fog, the horizon had shapes in the clouds, perhaps mountaintops. The gods had traveled the worlds in legends. *A portal?*

None that I have seen, Mistress.

I had heard the legends of the goddesses and gods traveling to other worlds. What world had I dropped into? We needed to get out of here and return to our world. My left arm and back burned, and the poison left me woozy. It would be a minute before I tried to stand. I'd survived this far. I was thirsty.

How long was I unconscious? I pushed up onto my right hand.

I can't tell time here. I'm disconnected. I don't know, Mistress.

I studied the gates. *Which gate did we come through?*

I'm not sure, Mistress.

A chill ran down my back. I flexed my left hand, fighting the pain. Some goddess, god, or power had built this cage. A trap for enemies or a transport for minions? So deep under the Minaoan Waste, it had to be ancient. I had to be careful. *I can't afford to end up somewhere worse. What do you mean by disconnected?*

Usually, I know where we are and can track your measurement of time and distance. Here, I have no such connection to our world, Mistress. A disturbing sense of panic shaded Khimmer's thoughts.

I was going to have to try one of these gates. The first time I'd entered, the world turned sideways for a moment. I took a deep breath and looked at the arch at my feet. It seemed the most likely guess. Assuming the gate let me out, I could use Khimmer to discern whether we were on the right world. If not, then reenter and try the next gate.

The patterns of the tiles extended from a central circle. The clouds masked any distinct shapes on the horizon. Just outside the gate, the pavers continued onto a ledge before stone met fog.

I took a deep breath and crouched at the arch; cautiously, I pressed my hand to the gate.

As before, I touched nothing, but shot through with my right side suddenly becoming down. The sky exploded into brilliant blue light. I fell sideways and flailed without hitting the ground.

Mistress! Nightarmor thickened around my body, and the helmet blocked my eyes before I connected with Khimmer's vision.

An impossible sun burned in the center of the sky. Treetops carpeted a hillside below me.

I was falling. Toppling in a slow spin, I saw the cliff's edge above from where I'd come, but no arch or gate. This world was not Duruce.

I hit a treetop with my back. Fragrant fir branches snapped under my weight. The sense of height tightened my chest. The sky disappeared, and green needles and branches enveloped me. Each brush against the tree jolted and spun me. Panic pushed through my poison-addled brain, and I grabbed at them, trying to find something to hold on to, or at least slow my fall.

Dread rose in my chest. Once, I'd jumped out of a window into a tall tree. That had been controlled. What I experienced this time was sheer mayhem.

A thicker branch caught the heel of my boot, and I jerked as it snapped. Another caught my chin and threw my head back. Somehow, my gauntleted hand caught a branch, and my body righted itself. My legs straightened and slowed. Momentary hope rose, then the wood snapped off in my grasp.

Impact, Mistress!

I saw the ground of brown needles through Khimmer's vision. Nightarmor filled out around me with braces between skin and plate. I tried to pull my legs in for the impact, but a thick branch caught my left arm. Pain shot through the wound on my back.

I slammed into the ground with my left leg first. Even in Nightarmor, I collapsed from the force and crumpled into a bed of needles. The forest floor tilted, and I rolled blindly as the world spun. I hadn't broken my leg.

Rolling into a tree trunk with my back, I sucked in a breath and found a moment to dig my heels into a pile of brown needles.

The world stopped moving. I stared up through the green filter of trees at a bright blue sky. The world smelled of pine and sap. The sun lay impossibly above. This could not be home. The sun on Duruce did not sit that high.

Where are we?

Khimmer did not answer. My chest hollowed with the sense of being alone.

Khimmer?

Mistress? I am nowhere. I do not know where we are. Khimmer sounded distracted.

I couldn't afford to get stuck in whatever world we'd landed on. Tilting my head back, I could see where the forest climbed up to a rocky rise. Brush grew in every nook. Too steep. Toxins still made my body weak. I would need another way up. *We've got to get back up to the top. To the gate.*

Khimmer did not respond. Were we on Duruce, Khimmer would know each mountain and how to approach it. I was on my own.

Agile.

Yes, Mistress.

I drew in the cool air as Nightarmor adjusted. A distant rumble sounded below. A rockslide? A beast of some sort? I leaned up and winced.

Khimmer pressed tight against my wound. From the placement of the bolt head, I doubted I could get it out on my own. Since I had not died yet, I had to assume that most of the poison had scraped off as it pierced Nightarmor. The toxin hadn't seemed to do more than make me sluggish and clumsy. Food and water would be important to recovery; then, an open wound and infection would be my concern. For all of that, I needed to get back to Duruce.

The forest stretched down to a black trail that cut through the trees like a river. A better vantage point would give me a sense of this mountain and its cliffs. The forest below seemed thinner, with more brush than trees and a less dangerous slope. The low growling sounded from that direction. I rose carefully and climbed downslope with my right hand trailing through the pine needles.

Whatever made the noise seemed to ebb and echo. There could have been more than one source. Two of them? I didn't relish finding some mammoth beasts like Manti-cores, or whatever this world offered. Nightarmor would protect me, but it might make my climb back up to the gate worrisome.

The trail below me had been made by someone. Finer than any city street, it had no seams or pavers. Black with embedded stones, it appeared as if poured and sunbaked akin to mortar. It held my weight as if stone itself.

In the distance, more than one creature whined and groaned around me. I had a better vantage here of the lower brush downhill, but the trees above still hid the mountaintop. I would walk along the path, if for nothing but the ease. At some point, I might get a view of the slope and plot a path up. I wanted to rest. Thirst would be my downfall. I heard no sound of water, only the damnable beasts.

I passed a patch where the new world's sun cut through the canopy and marked the ground. The road cut a deep tunnel through the forest, most of it shrouded in shadows.

Even in agile form, Nightarmor chafed. One of the beasts sounded closer, and I turned, searching the winding path. A glint, as if from metal or eyes, showed in the darkness that the trail and surrounding trees formed.

Are you coming for me?

Mistress?

I crouched, squinting though I saw through Khimmer's vision. The beast didn't creep. Large, with glowing white eyes, it raced toward me down the black path. Faster than any buck or fox, it had twice the mass of any long-haired, grazing Ure. It spotted me. I could make for the forest or stand my ground on level terrain. I reached back for my sword, and Khimmer formed it so the hilt shoved into my gauntlet.

Battle armor.

Yes, Mistress. Nightarmor thickened.

I drew a deep breath. Colored gray, the creature had no fur. It shone unnaturally, as if made of metal or glass. It didn't lope or run. Gliding like a low flying bird, it hugged the trail with a persistent growl.

I waited for it with my sword pointed. Apprehension built as the size grew. It moved impossibly fast. Backing toward the edge of the forest, I prepared to dodge, slice, and run in among the trees. Its size would be a disadvantage there, and certainly it couldn't maintain its speed.

A distinctly human head emerged out of the side of the beast. Hair blowing, a man with a mustache smiled at me and whooped as he approached. Another male, sitting behind glass laughed. It was no beast but a carriage, rolling on thick black wheels but without an animal to pull. Magic of some sort.

They screeched as they roared past, turning along the trail. The carriage wailed a mournful note.

I turned with its passing and found a second carriage upon me. Tall and white, it screeched and wailed as well. A man and woman sat before a large window flush to the front. As it sped around the corner, it swerved and tilted its square shape. I dodged, but it bore down upon me.

Mistress!

My head slammed inside my helmet. I'd never felt such an impact. I bounced into the air. Pain burned across my left side and hip. The air and trees spun above. Nightarmor's metal screeched as I skidded off the hard trail. Stars lit an already bright sky.

The squealing of the carriage echoed inside Nightarmor's helmet. I rolled into the grass and brush, unable to move.

Mistress?

My head throbbed. My sight ebbed. I lingered at the edge of consciousness. *My sword.* Distorted sounds rolled in my helmet. The beast — the carriage — rumbled nearby, not moving.

Your sword is on the trail, Mistress. Is your head damaged? People approach.

I wanted to retch. *Yes, I'm hurt.* My head swam at the consideration of sitting up. The fire under my arm added to the bruise that had become the left side of my body. Voices drifted in the confusion of noises around me. I could not defend myself, but unless they had a Blessed Blade, Nightarmor would protect me.

A shadowy silhouette knelt beside me. They spoke a strange language. Female.

What language?

This is no language I can help you with, Mistress. I will study it, but it links to nothing that I know.

A second shape approached, then a third. An angry male spoke harsh words. I tensed, but waited. If they were hostile, Nightarmor would protect me. I was certainly on one of the mythical worlds. They were always described as violent places. I flexed my fingers and muscles, discerning how much movement I would have — if needed. Pain accompanied every motion.

The larger shadow of the three resolved into a stern looking man. He seemed my age, mid to late twenties. His face was clean shaven with a distinct chin and golden-orange hair that was coiffed into the air like a horse's mane. He asked a question of the woman with an angry tone.

My heart beat quicker, anticipating an attack. I could move my right arm. However, my left arm with my short blade sheathed on the forearm rested by my side, resisting any movement. I would have to reach across my body to get to it. As bruised as I felt, it would not be a graceful task. After that, I doubted I could stand. My toes moved, but the left leg resisted even tightening its thigh muscles.

The taller, thinner figure was a woman with long, black hair. She pushed him away and asked gentler questions. Her tone calmed my pulse. The woman smiled with full lips and dark eyes as she spoke.

Truth.

Something the woman had said triggered my truthsense. What had it been?

My head throbbed, and I kept flexing my legs; my left side ached, but nothing seemed broken. My hopes of climbing the mountain drained away, and apprehension tightened my chest. Somehow, I had to get to the top of the ridge, back to the gates.

Mistress, you have to heal. You can't climb in this condition. We shall surely fall.

Shh.

I scraped my right elbow back, trying to sit up. My vision spun, and the ground appeared to swallow me.

The third figure leaned in with thin lips and shadows painted under their eyes. Flat chested, they were likely a male, but their features were delicate enough to be a woman's. A ring pierced their nose like the Mindarins. Speaking a single word three times, each time tapping their chest, they pointed at me and waited. "Tyler."

Was that some type of name? I listened to the exchange, an odd language, but in it I did hear the woman use the word when she addressed the wiry person.

I think their name is Tyler.

I concur, Mistress.

The angry man had returned with my sword, but he didn't offer it to me; instead, he leaned the point into the ground. I managed to stay up on an elbow this time, blinking away the lights that sparkled in my vision.

Mistress?

He has my sword.

He cannot harm you with it, Mistress. I will absorb it if he brings it close.

Feebly, I reached for the tip of the sword. The exchange among the three strangers became heated. A few lies and some truths scattered through their words so quickly I could not be sure who spoke them.

I don't like this. I have to get up. I bent my left knee despite the pain, but the dizziness overwhelmed me.

They became excited at my struggle and Tyler made the angry man place the sword on top of me. I laid back down, clasping it. I couldn't get up yet.

They moved to each side of me. The angry man seemed to swear as he struggled to get his arms under Nightarmor. I attempted to struggle. Tyler aided weakly from my opposite side. The woman took hold of Nightarmor's boots.

Whoever they are, I do not believe they mean you harm, Mistress. Further harm.

They managed to get me off the ground. My head spun, and I stifled the urge to retch inside Nightarmor's helmet. I might be able to move, but until my head stopped spinning, I wouldn't be walking anywhere on my own. Shuffling, they carried me to a large opening in the carriage. The woman set down my feet and climbed in ahead of us, easing my head inside.

Perhaps they have a healer, Mistress.

Whatever they intended, I was at their mercy. My side and joints had swelled, but my head was the largest betrayal. I needed rest and water. A large panel slid noisily and sealed the opening.

Panic flared in my chest at the sound.

If they could take me to a healer, then the sooner I would be on my way back to the mountain. Perhaps they had an estate nearby. I tried not to imagine more nefarious purposes. If they did intend me harm, they likely would have tried already. Possibly, these were only servants who would bring me to their liege. Until my head stopped throbbing and I could move properly, I would have to go along with them.

The carriage had large seats with gray, padded cushions and metal frames that rose out of the floor. Gray glass lined the sides near the top. *What magic propels this carriage?*

Unknown, Mistress.

I had little choice in the matter, so I rested my head on the floor and stared up at the white ribbing of the ceiling. The air had odd scents which could have been strange food. They continued to talk and argue. I hoped that Khimmer would be able to translate soon.

As the carriage whined into motion, Nightarmor rattled on the metal floor. Tyler sat beside me and spoke. I had no idea what was said, but they were truths.

Holding my sword on my breastplate, I flexed every muscle and joint that I could. My body swelled at my left hip, but it wasn't broken. My head, though, floated between pain and near unconsciousness.

The angry man sat at the front, steering the carriage with a large wheel like the sailing ships upon the Esyx River. He argued and often lied. The woman's long hair hung over the back of the seat in front of me. They hardly seemed a threat, but they were taking me away from the gates.

Khimmer, will you be able to return us here?

Theoretically, Mistress.

Tyler seemed engrossed and energetic in their discourse. Certain words repeated frequently. It would be a while before I'd gain any sense of their language; it didn't resemble anything from my world. Khimmer would grasp it quicker, and translation would be better than being left in the dark.

My pulse relaxed with the movement, and Tyler's voice had a soothing quality.

I closed my eyes and held my sword against Nightarmor. *What is Tyler talking about?*

If I were to guess, Mistress, themselves. The base language does seem simple.

I opened my eyes and sucked in a breath. I wanted them to understand that I needed healing and couldn't leave the vicinity of the mountain. *You understand it?*

No, Mistress, but certain verbs are overused, and their inflexion is simplistic to non-existent, while intonation is relied upon heavily.

I relaxed, resigned. *But, you don't understand it.*

Not yet. Not well enough to translate, Mistress.

I focused on the windows. Their carriage cut through oaks, winding along what I assumed was the same trail. Coaxed by Tyler's gentle voice, I found myself tired and drifting toward sleep.

When two other carriages passed, going in the opposite direction with a flurry of sound, I startled awake. Any calm which Tyler brought with words disappeared as my heart raced.

How far have we traveled, Khimmer? I couldn't get too far from the gate.

Eighteen leagues, Mistress.

It would take half a day of walking to return. I arched my back to rise and found my neck stiff. My thoughts fogged, and my vision swam. Thirst dried my throat. I relaxed and again worked through my muscles and joints. The tip of the crossbow bolt burned in my shoulder. Tyler spoke in a soothing voice while the other two argued.

When their carriage came to a stop, I managed to get my right elbow under myself and pushed up. Tyler motioned for me to remain. The rumbling stopped, and the angry man opened his door and stepped out. The woman leaned over and asked questions of Tyler and possibly myself. The tops of green tents showed through the window to my right. A market of some sort?

Can you tell what she asked?

No, Mistress. But I do believe the other man is called John based on the word placement and repetition.

That's an odd name.

She left, and I leaned higher, but could only see the tents and trees on a hillside.

It could be a derivation of Jiannis.

My head felt less heavy. The headache pounded, but the sparkles in my vision had stopped. I should get out now and head back to the mountain. A healer could help with the tip of the crossbow bolt and bind the wound. Nightarmor's compression and the myriad other bruises helped hide the pain, but it would need tending. I needed water. Perhaps they had an open well at the market.

I startled when the door opened again. John and the woman had brought food. The smell of fried foods filled the carriage, both nauseating me and making me hungry. They had brought cups as well. I could barely fight my thirst. Did I dare trust them? Perhaps this had all been a ruse to poison me. The carriage rumbled, and they moved on from the market.

Tyler offered me one of their beverages, but I kept Nightarmor's helmet sealed. I could smell sweet fruit.

The three ate and drank while I watched through Khimmer's vision.

Mistress, I believe the woman and John are discussing you.

How do you know? I leaned to the right, focusing on them.

I believe they are calling you a soldier.

I stiffened at the slur. We had left wars behind us.

I do not understand the complete context, thought Khimmer.

Translate as best as you can. I tried to ignore Tyler.

Mistress, it would be partial and incorrect.

Do it.

As you wish, Mistress.

John, one hand holding a loose pie of some sort, spoke in a harsh tone with the woman.

Do with soldier? thought Khimmer.

They had no plan for me yet. No healer.

The woman spoke, including Tyler's name. *Truth.*

They have some concern for Tyler's safety, suggested Khimmer.

John burst into a tirade. *Truths.*

Tyler stopped talking and drooped.

John is concerned for their safety. He blames Tyler. You are a risk. I could be wrong, Mistress. I believe their destination is named Venice.

The woman's tone sharpened, a rebuke. *Truth.*

She believes you are in danger, Mistress.

How? I shifted the sword and pushed up to a sitting position.

I don't know, Mistress.

The woman looked back to me and forced a smile. She spoke again to John in a persuasive tone. *Truth.*

She wishes to take you to a place called hospital. There are risks. It seems she fears for your health either way.

I did need a healer. If there were risks, then it would be

better to find the gate and return. I'd find help in Vale Aganor. I felt like I was six again, being led around the dark Aegis monastery halls, oblivious to what lay around the corner.

I can't take that risk.

I will tell you what to say, Mistress. We should be able to gauge if my interpretation is correct from their reaction.

Remove my helmet. I took a deep breath as Nightarmor melted off my head.

Tyler jerked back with a gasp. John turned in his seat, dropping his food.

"Not hospital," I said.

CHAPTER 15

Earth

The carriage screeched and veered toward the trees. The wheels below me hit rough terrain, bouncing me with a clank against the floor. I used my right hand to brace myself. Trees loomed, and the carriage skidded to a stop.

The woman jumped out immediately while John wrestled with a lever at the front. Tyler shifted away from me with wide eyes. Their hands searched behind them for purchase before Tyler found the handle to the wide, sliding door. It shrieked as it opened. My pulse raced.

I'm not sure your translation is correct.

Perhaps, Mistress.

Panicked, Tyler joined the others standing in the grass staring in at me and arguing wildly.

They are concerned, Mistress.

That is obvious.

Tyler's reaction hurt, for no good reason. I did not know

these people. I took a deep breath. Had they been disconcerted by Nightarmor shifting, or what I said?

I believe the woman's name is Deanna. She considers you a greater risk now, Mistress. John believes he might have to fight you.

I snorted at the idea of the bulky man attacking me without armor or a weapon. *They might never have seen Nightarmor before.* Head pounding, I shifted my legs out the opening.

That is likely, Mistress. I am the last one serving.

I'd made a mistake letting them take me. I thought they had been intending to take me to a healer. Their version of one, at least. I held my sword and tested my legs on the ground. I'd been dazed. The fight on the Minaoan Waste, the poison, the fall from the gate, and the impact with the carriage had left me thinking improperly. Sword tip pressed into the grass, I stood better than I expected. *We've got to get back to the mountain. Can you guide me back?*

Yes, Mistress. Khimmer hesitated, not seeming confident.

Tyler's fear saddened me. They had befriended me; now they felt betrayed. Whatever danger they faced, I hoped they did well.

I jerked stiff as a dark blue carriage, low like the first I'd seen, skidded into the grass behind us. Two bearded men sat inside. The passenger leaned and shoved a long piece of equipment out the window.

Nightarmor flowed up into a helmet over my head and thickened across my chest. *Eldritch weapons, Mistress! Run!*

The man pointed first at Tyler and the others, then adjusted to aim at me as if he held a crossbow.

Explosions rattled out of the weapon. Fiery bursts flickered from the nozzle. Metal stones slammed into

Nightarmor causing me to stagger back. My heart raced. Heat burned my chest. Even through the helmet, I was deafened.

I dropped into a crouch, but the attacker had already swept the weapon toward the others. The violence of the weapon had stunned me momentarily, and Nightarmor reformed. My teeth clenched with anger. I'd had enough of a disastrous morning with assassins, strange gates, and the magic carriages of this world. I would not let these men hurt Tyler.

Mistress!

I ran at the carriage, even as the passenger moved the exploding weapon toward me. He frowned with deeply furrowed eyebrows. He had not expected me to survive. Throwing my shoulder forward, I jumped at the flat front of the carriage, bracing for the pain of my wound. I held Khimmer's sword tucked across my front. Metal from the Eldritch weapon clattered against Nightarmor's helmet, and I felt the heat.

The second man, at the steering wheel, raised a smaller weapon.

The carriage groaned under the impact of my shoulder. I barely noticed the burn of the wound on my back. Nightarmor swam around me, keeping the thickest side toward the attackers.

The window shattered as a sharper explosion cracked from inside the carriage.

Rolling, I used the momentum to drive Khimmer's sword through the remnants of glass and into the passenger's heart. My head swam, but I shifted to my left hip. Through the new opening, I drove my heel into the neck of the man at the steering wheel. Bones cracking, he slumped.

The stars had returned to my vision. I shifted off their carriage clumsily, feeling the toll of my sudden movements.

Mistress?

Okay. Dizzy. I forced my right leg to hold me steady, but leaned against the still rumbling carriage. My left leg failed, and I slid down to one knee, propped up with Khimmer's sword. My back and hips throbbed. The trees appeared to tilt.

The others had fled. Their carriage grumbled in the grass. Without armor, they might have been killed by the Eldritch weapons. I needed to check.

Khimmer highlighted their body heat, hiding or dying in the shrubs and grass. They moved. John first, who lifted his head to watch me. Tyler and the woman followed.

I could do little more than keep myself from falling onto the ground.

Jumping up, John began yelling. His eyes locked on me.

Mistress, I believe he blames Tyler for the attack. These men were following Tyler.

Tyler ignored John and rose to approach me.

I pushed to get my left leg up. Deanna crouched in the grass, watching me with wide eyes. Tyler spoke quietly, even as John raged.

Tyler questions your health, Mistress.

I straightened, despite my pounding head. *Remove my helmet.* Nightarmor poured off my face. Using Khimmer's translation, I hopefully said, "I am unharmed, Tyler."

It appeared proper, as Tyler offered his hand to help me rise. I would have rather rested in the grass, but I took his hand in Nightarmor's gauntlet and pulled myself to stand.

Deanna rose, suddenly urgent, and moved for their carriage. She spoke swiftly, ignoring John's angry words.

John barked out comments as he too moved for the carriage.

Only Tyler remained, standing beside me, and spoke quietly to the other two, causing them to pause.

All truths.

It seems, Mistress, Tyler intends for you to continue with them. The other two intend to leave you.

I looked behind us at the path we'd been traveling. Hills and woods blocked any view of the horizon beyond that. Without healing, rest, and water, I wouldn't be able to walk long. Climbing would be impossible.

I need to tell them I must heal and return to the gate, to the forest where they found me. Khimmer translated and I stumbled through the awkward foreign words.

Tyler listened to me and then shook their head, pointing to the carriage with the two attackers I had killed. Tyler spoke softly even as the others yelled.

Tyler believes that more of these people, their enemy I believe, will be searching, and perhaps for you now. Others too, perhaps guards. It does not sound safe here, Mistress.

Is it any safer to go?

Perhaps for now, Mistress.

Deanna and John remained by their carriage, yelling at Tyler.

Tyler believes it is fate that you were here, or they would have died on the road.

John yelled, but Tyler replied quietly and calmly, and they seemed at an impasse. Traveling with them to a healer would be the best option.

I can be a bit intimidating, Mistress. These people do not seem a threat. Should you risk reducing me?

They were not my enemy. John disliked me, based on his behavior, and Deanna perhaps feared me.

I took a deep breath and placed the sword on Nightarmor's back to let Khimmer absorb it. Leaving only my black leggings and tunic, Nightarmor reduced to bracelets, boots, belt, gorget, and pauldrons. The latter kept pressure over the wound where the crossbow bolt was lodged into my flesh.

Tyler shifted slightly as Nightarmor drizzled away, leaving our fingers touching. They stopped talking and studied me. Their eyebrows dropped as they noted the blood matting the side of my tunic.

Deanna and John turned silent as Tyler led me back toward the carriage. I couldn't know that they would honor my request, but I needed healing first. If there were more enemies here with Eldritch weapons, then I needed to be in better shape to handle them.

John snapped out a few biting comments and marched off for his door. Deanna watched me, her face drawn in with a concerned expression.

I glanced back at the dead attackers in their carriage and the wooded ridges. Had it been fate that I had been here? I would have to return, healed and in disguise.

CHAPTER 16

Slovenia - Earth

Tyler tried to get me to rest on the floor again, but instead I sat on one of the benches, and they sat beside me. The carriage moved at a remarkable speed. Deanna and John avoided me after the first few glances. They spoke quietly now and infrequently.

I drank from Tyler's cup. It had a brown color like over-steeped tea, but smelled and tasted like fruit and sugar with harsh bubbles. I needed water. Blisters had formed in some spots where the Eldritch weapons had hit Nightarmor. My left hip swelled.

Tyler asked me a question. Their intonations did seem to dominate their language.

I waited for Khimmer to translate. I'd learned Silari living among the people while Khimmer trained me. This would be more difficult because we were both learning the language. Getting back to the gate would take more effort than I had planned.

Tyler wishes to know your name, Mistress.

I thought about the question, as no one on this world would know of my position with Queen Meihlia. "Ahnjii," I said.

Tyler smiled and pointed to their chest and Khimmer translated.

Tyler Ramnath, they, them.

I don't understand, Khimmer.

They and them are pronouns, Mistress. Perhaps they identify as some of the Helios acolytes do, without gender. I am unsure what the title Ramnath means.

I had not assumed Tyler's gender. It would not be wise to give my title of First Assassin of Queen Meihlia, not until I understood this world better.

"Ahnjii Fate." I smiled at using Tyler's own definition of me. "She, her."

Their laugh pleased me. Tyler straightened their expression and spoke.

Tyler wishes to know where you are from, Mistress.

"Vale Aganor," I answered.

Tyler wrinkled their forehead and shrugged. They did not know of my home. I had not known of theirs until a few hours ago. Obviously the legends were true of these other worlds, but perhaps with the gate so remote on the cliffs, these people had lost all knowledge of it. The counterpart, under the Minaoan Waste, had certainly been forgotten by my people. Would the Queen send someone to search for me? Would she find the gate as well?

Khimmer helped me translate a question. "Where you are from?"

"Tallahassee, in Florida."

Tyler had a gentle demeanor, but their eyes seemed to

note every movement and studied my expressions. Hand on my forearm, they wrinkled their brow and spoke.

Tyler wants to know if your home is in Slovenia, Mistress. If you are a soldier there?

I swallowed, stinging at the bite of the slur. It might be a translation mistake. "No." I did not need Khimmer to respond.

Tyler raised their eyebrows and tapped on Nightarmor's pauldron.

Tyler says you wear armor, Mistress. I did not understand their description. Sorry. Only a soldier would wear armor. They likely have never seen Nightarmor. They might consider it magical.

Tyler's confusion made a little more sense. I can't tell them I was an assassin. In this situation, I needed to be careful, as if in a foreign land. "Not soldier."

John glanced up to look in the mirror at my comment. I had spoken forcefully. I hadn't liked the insult.

Tyler jerked a thumb behind and spoke.

Tyler says you kill like a soldier, Mistress. You protected them from the enemies that hunted Tyler.

Why did someone hunt Tyler? I frowned, but Tyler continued motioning to Deanna.

Deanna is their sister, and she came here to free Tyler. They are traveling home. You are welcome to join them.

I did not need a home. I needed a healer.

Deanna called out sharply to Tyler. John grumbled and glared in the mirror.

She does not agree to Tyler's offer, Mistress.

Can you get us back to the gate?

Likely, Mistress. I've been recording our path, but I have no reference points or connection with this world.

Tyler argued with the other two with a calm, glib tone.

John yelled, causing Tyler to smirk. In some way, it was satisfying.

I leaned back, still thirsty after the beverage. The wound would infect if I let it. The carriage smelled of fried foods and an acrid odor I could not place. We passed farmlands with unusual equipment and carriages. Barns grew to the size of city blocks. I still had not learned the name of this strange world.

Tyler had called it fate that I was there to save them. While I was trapped here, King Dior had been given a reprieve. I had a duty to the Queen, Goddess Nyx, and Vale Aganor, despite the betrayal against myself and family. Forcing myself to care about my mission, I had Khimmer translate a statement.

"I need a healer to tend my wound. I need to return to the mountain where you found me."

Arguments blossomed among them without any direct response to me.

They are concerned about the enemy searching for Tyler and believe the carriage has been identified. John wishes to leave you. Deanna believes they need to help find you a healer. Tyler wishes for you to leave this place before anyone can hurt you, Mistress.

I gave up trying to explain my plight to them and shifted to find some comfort on the padded bench. The three of them ranged from anger to fear. My wound would take me if I did not have it tended. Without proper salves, small wounds killed, and I still had the tip of the crossbow bolt inside my flesh.

The three still argued when John slowed the carriage and pulled into a large but sparsely populated marketplace. A small building with a wall of glass sat in the back. Huge pillars supported a long canopy. Another carriage parked underneath attached to some equipment by a long black hose.

John barked and jumped out of the carriage. Tyler asked a question of Deanna as they got up for the door.

Tyler wants her to take you to bathe, Mistress.

I looked at the building. It hardly looked like a bath-house. Could there be a healer here? The people here wore such bright costumes, like nobles or priestesses of Phylloa. I could see for myself and did not need Deanna. Tyler stood outside where the warm air carried a sharp scent, like paint. Their sun had moved, no longer directly overhead.

Deanna rubbed her breastbone with a grimace as I exited. I dressed oddly for this culture; I would stand out. She sighed and quickly stepped out of her door with a sheepish smile, gesturing for me to follow. We crossed the black paved market.

I followed her into a common latrine that smelled of urine and citrus. Odd lamps without flame lit the ceiling. The toilets were porcelain and hidden in closets. The sinks had no water in the basins. Large mirrors covered the walls. I would need water and bandages. I saw neither.

Do you know the words for bandage or water? I asked Khimmer.

No, Mistress. Sorry.

Deanna studied me, then moved to a basin and turned a metal handle. Water poured out steadily with no pump in sight. The urge to pee grew strong at the sound. I drank handfuls before heading to a toilet where water waited in the bottom.

I did not understand this strange world. Their wood looked polished, yet worn and chipped. Deanna chose a different stall and locked herself inside.

The tip of the crossbow bolt would have to come out. *Do you believe they are taking me to a healer, Khimmer?*

Not directly, Mistress. They argue over that point.

I returned to the basin and stared at myself in the mirror. The exposed skin on my left side had turned purple.

Water rushed inside Deanna's stall, but the floor remained mostly dry. She unlocked the door and emerged to wash her hands with a fragrant, lathering lotion from a box in the wall. From another, she pulled sheaves of thick paper to dry her hands. It would have to do.

Undress.

Nightarmor minimized the belt while the pauldrons and gorget formed into thin jewelry. I pulled off the tunic, tossed it into a basin, and turned the handle; the water turned pink from blood. My left side had one continuous bruise from the tops of my leggings up my side and down my arm.

Without Nightarmor's compression, the wound on my right shoulder began seeping blood. Deanna backed away, her face paling. I rinsed off what dried blood I could and soaked the back of my leggings in the process.

I imagined fingertips for a glove to Khimmer. Using the mirror, I leaned against the counter and dug into the wound. Blood trickled out readily. I plucked at a splintered stump from the crossbow bolt head. My stomach soured at the pain, but I locked onto the end, and Khimmer tightened the grip.

With a gasp, I pulled it out. Metal clattered to the yellow stained floor. Deanna cried out and held both hands to her lips. I held onto the counter with both hands despite the blood trickling down my back. The pain threatened to blacken my vision.

Mistress?

Remove the glove.

The glove dissolved back up to my bracelet.

Deanna spoke. She looked as queasy as I felt.

She wishes to help, Mistress.

I nodded weakly.

Timidly at first, she washed the wound area with lotion and paper. Biting her lip and holding a wad of paper against my wound, she cleaned me better than I had. A healer might have had numbing salve.

Deanna obviously had misgivings about my continued presence with them, but she helped with careful compassion.

She paused once I had been washed and she'd placed a new wad of dry paper over my wound. I took the makeshift bandage from her. *Pauldron.*

Nightarmor spread a thin decorative armor over my shoulders. The pressure hurt, then numbed some of the pain.

I squeezed out my tunic while Deanna wiped blood from the floor and counters. I would still need a healer for a proper bandage and poultice, but this was better.

I wish to thank her.

I don't know those words yet, Mistress.

I nodded and smiled, took a last drink while wishing for a proper water bag, and headed for the door.

Deanna chortled, and I turned back to her. Her face flushing, she motioned to her chest and then mine.

Reluctantly, I slid the wet tunic on and covered my chest. That appeared to placate her. Nightarmor slid down and formed an ornate belt about my waist. Khimmer had their own sense of decorum when it came to dressing.

I staggered outside, assaulted by new foul smells. This

world had sharp, acrid scents. Their sun was too bright and yellow, and I squinted.

A man scowled at us at first, then smiled. I waved. Deanna pressed my hand down and laughed as she steered us toward John's carriage.

Tyler had a pile of strange foods and beverages. A cold tea proved palatable, and I tried the items offered as we drove. A spicy cracker proved appealing. The toxins still had me nauseous, so I ate sparingly. The buildings grew taller and closer together as we drove.

Khimmer, in all the legends, have you ever heard of such a place?

During and before the wars, our own world had such oddities, Mistress.

Deanna and John spoke in hushed voices at the front. He still argued against whatever she proposed, but she seemed firm in this conviction.

What are they talking about?

You, Mistress. Deanna and Tyler intend to take you to a place called Tallahassee.

Is this good?

I do not know, Mistress. You will need to rest and heal. The temperature around your wound is rising. It will become infected without a healer or proper salve.

Whatever town they had entered stretched on endlessly. Impossibly tall buildings rose on the horizon. John slowed us at a strange metallic fence where many strange carriages waited. Some were many times longer than what we rode, with a rounded and bulbous shape, pointed fronts, and small circular windows.

My chest tightened with anxiety as we came to a stop at a guard's shack. Deanna leaned over and spoke to the guard there, showing him some picture on a shiny card.

Is this Tallahassee? Perhaps they had healers here.

I do not know, Mistress. The letters on the sign are strange to me.

John drove forward and pulled in beside a fence. Tyler gathered his bags of food and beverages while Deanna hopped out to go meet with a uniformed man — not a guard, but a liveried servant it appeared.

What is going on?

I do not know, Mistress. I do not believe she spoke in the same language to the guard.

Tyler gestured for me to follow, and I felt some reluctance. The three seemed excited, but I didn't know about what.

With Khimmer's help, I asked, "Where?" I stepped out cautiously.

Tyler pointed toward one of the strange carriages. Stairs poked out of it. Large boards of metal extended from the side. "Tallahassee."

I had trusted Tyler so far. The liveried servant watched me with a frown as I followed Tyler to the new carriage. The inside could have been the cabin of a sailing ship with the small windows. The padded chairs and mounted tables would have rivaled the lavish sitting room of the Silarin Ambassador.

John seemed too tall for the room, but his demeanor indicated he had relaxed. Tyler settled me into a chair and sat beside me. A liveried servant appeared from a back door and brought beverages in crystal glasses. Were Tyler and these people nobles? Why had they been traveling in the first carriage without servants?

I believe, Mistress, they are going home. Tallahassee. I cannot understand what they are saying to the servants; they speak a different language.

Tyler leaned over and picked up a belt at my waist. They pointed it toward another strap with metal. I was able to clasp the two ends together with a click, locking me into the chair. I took a tight breath. I trusted Tyler.

I do too, Mistress.

The energy among the three spoke of relief or happiness. Whatever dilemma they had been embroiled in had likely ended. Tyler had been the focus of it. What had they done to cause people to want to kill Tyler?

The carriage began to groan and whine. The servants moved quicker as we rolled forward. I couldn't see much through the little window, but we were alone on a massive field of the black pavement. We began to go too fast, and I could feel the pressure in my bones.

Tyler smiled when I searched their face.

"Tallahassee?" I asked.

The walls spoke around me, ending with the same word. Had I made a mistake going with them? Tyler laughed as I held my breath. Chest tight, I could see only blue sky outside the windows. The buildings had disappeared. I glanced at the window on the other side of Tyler. The ground dwindled below.

Impact! I thought to Khimmer.

Nightarmor poured around me in protection.

Tyler startled as if surprised, then a lazy grin cut across their face. They laughed and spoke.

Tyler believes you do not need Nightarmor, Mistress. In fact, you should not show it to others.

I glanced out the window again, shuddered, then focused on Tyler. *Remove armor, Khimmer.* It would take me a while to get used to this strange world. Once the risk of infection passed, I'd have to go back and find the gate.

CHAPTER 17

RAILROAD SQUARE ART DISTRICT, Tallahassee - Earth

Weeks later, I sat at Fat Cat Books and coaxed a black cat into my lap. The bookstore had a fragrant scent, as if they'd gotten more candles or potpourri delivered. I sipped zesty tea from the Square Mug Café. Vivianne held the cup I'd brought her in her too long fingers.

"Are you married?" I asked Vivianne.

She scoffed and lifted her cup. "How old do I look?" Vivianne smiled over the lid.

I hadn't thought we were much different. "My age," I guessed.

Taking a languishing sip, she held a sly smile. "Twice that. I wouldn't consider marriage this young. Some do, just not me. You really are a strange witch."

Digging nails through the cat's short fur, I didn't ask any more questions. My failed trip with Deanna to Slovenia in search of the portal had given me time to consider my future here on Earth. Tyler had suggested I not let anyone else know about my origins. Asking questions when a witch should know the answer only highlighted my naïveté about Earth.

"I can't see myself getting married." With my training ingrained from the Aegis Monks, I couldn't imagine having a relationship. Friends were new for me.

"How about that college boy you met here?" She tilted her head with a grin as if waiting for me to answer.

I liked Vivianne and she appeared to like talking with me. Outside of Tyler, she was the only other friend I'd made on Earth. I talked with the servers when I got boba tea, or Pete at the Crum Box, but chatting with Vivianne was as personal as I got with Tyler. The red-haired boy had been no more than an interesting night.

"He was fun once. I didn't answer any of his texts afterward."

Vivianne rolled her eyes. "Give them a week or two at least. I do." She leaned forward, more serious. "I'll find someone who I want to get serious with; so will you."

I couldn't tell her about the fear that rose just thinking about an actual relationship. Explaining my concerns would lead to a conversation which we couldn't have. Finishing my tea, I placed it on the small table between us.

We were talking about a date she'd had with another Fae when Tyler messaged me.

"Pho? Thirty minutes?"

I sent him a smiling head emoji. "Yes!"

"Bookstore?" Tyler knew of my Saturday morning visits to Vivianne.

"Yes." I lifted the phone. "Tyler's picking me up for lunch."

She raised both eyebrows. "Have you?"

I scoffed. "No. Tyler's a friend."

We gave up our seats when customers arrived to pet the cats more than look at books. I was leaning on the counter when Tyler arrived to pick me up. Vivianne gave me a sly smile, greeted Tyler, and headed to her customers.

As we stepped into the heat, Tyler jerked a thumb over their shoulder. "You're friend always smiles like you two have some secret."

I could respond to that comment honestly. "Because we do." Not telling Tyler about the Fae bothered me, but it was Vivianne's secret, not mine.

Tyler unlocked the car and peered around before speaking. "She doesn't know about the gate and all that, does she?"

"No." I slid into the seat of the warm Prius and pulled down the harness. "You warned me about that."

"And . . ." Tyler gestured to their neck and arms, indicating my Nightarmor jewelry.

I shook my head. Even Deanna had sternly warned me about not having anyone see my armor. It had been the last time she mentioned it.

Tyler turned to watch the road as they backed up. "There are governments and corporations that would kill to learn your secrets. If they knew you came from someplace off world, the CIA would dissect you."

"Deanna said the KGB would cut me open to understand my armor." Khimmer had not believed the process would work, but suggested I avoid the situation.

Tyler frowned lightly. "When did she say that? During your trip to Slovenia? You don't seem as depressed as I thought you might be — for not finding your gate."

Deanna had appeared relieved when we couldn't find anything. I had been upset, but mostly because I didn't really want to leave Earth and Tyler. "I'll try again. I needed more time. The ridge is much longer than it looks on the internet."

Tyler drove in silence for a while, tapping their finger on the steering wheel though they hadn't put on music. When they spoke, they didn't take their eyes off the road. "I can't say I'm disappointed you didn't find your way home. I like having you here."

I smiled, looking out the window so Tyler wouldn't see.

We were passing a small market of buildings with cars parked all the way up to the sidewalk. A young woman in greens and blues walked in the opposite direction. She had longer hair than Vivianne but the same blonde color and the same tall ears. A Fae.

I didn't yell out her secret to Tyler, nor even turn my head much as we passed. She looked happy in her day, not worrying that someone like me could tell who she was. I tilted my head, leaning against the window, and grinned. "I think I like being here, too."

Please head to my website and join my mailing list if you'd like to be kept up to date on this series or my other books.

Khimmer Chronicles

Wight's Wrath - Book One

Death's Contract - Book Two

Fate's Betrayal - Book Three

High Fae's Quest - Book Four

Friday's Fifth - Book Five

Nyx's Blade - The Origin Story

AngelSong Series

Penumbra - Book One

Red Tempest - Book Two

Coerced - Book Three

Demons' Lair - Book Four

Infrared - Book Five

If you haven't read the Origin story of the **AngelSong** series, *Shattered Blood*, then download a free ebook or purchase the paperback or audible on Amazon.

Website KevinArthurDavis.com

Facebook @KevinArthurDavis

KevinADavis on Instagram

KevinADavisUF on Twitter

Playing with the end of my braid, I blew out a long breath, trying to calm my nerves. I straightened the straps of my bodysuit, then opened the creaking door to William Buford's office.

Human, like myself, he had paler skin, looked older than I'd expected, and wore a loose black suit. Smiling warmly, he rose from behind his desk. An open book rested with a pen left in the spine, perhaps to keep his place. Wavy, short hair hung above his ears. I couldn't tell if he'd forgotten to shave or if he kept his gray speckled fuzz along the chin fashionably trimmed. The room smelled like fried rice from the night before, unless that was his breakfast. My stomach growled.

I stuck out my hand in proper Earth, or at least Tallahassee, tradition. "Ahnjii Fate; I'm here for the interview."

He smiled, pumped my hand, and studied me as he spoke. "William Buford; call me Bill." Letting go of my hand, he pointed to a padded chair and dropped back into his own seat. His nose appeared round and thick. "Ms. Fate, I've been told you have peculiar talents."

Everyone had been clear to keep my abilities secret, but my friend Deanna had set up the job for me and I trusted her opinions when it came to staying out of trouble. I needed a job and did horribly in retail — it got boring real quick. She'd said that she knew a defense attorney who wouldn't want anyone knowing what I could do, if he hired me. My secret would be safe.

"Yes. I can tell when someone's lying," I said. The Aegis monks had called it truthsense, but the name didn't matter.

He pursed his lips and leaned forward, nodding. "You won't be offended if I test that statement, would you?"

"Go for it." I forced my smile down, once I realized I was grinning.

His expression turned bland and nonchalant. "I didn't like Deadpool's humor."

Lie. The thought and feeling were as sure as if I'd lied myself. The wrongness hung in his voice and in the air between us. "That's a lie," I said quickly. Who was Deadpool?

"My daughter likes bunnies."

Truth. "True."

"I didn't have a crush on Melody."

Lie. I detected seven more of his deadpan statements with my truthsense.

His expression grew more serious as we parried back and forth until he finally threw his hands up and laughed. "You're hired. Pay is twenty an hour. Probably eight or ten hours a week, more if I'm in a trial. Otherwise, depositions and jury selection." He paused, touching his lips with a fingertip. "Don't know how you do it."

"Sounds great. Thank you." Deanna had said to ask for fifty dollars an hour, but Bill seemed so excited, I just couldn't.

He stood and reached out to shake my hand again. I had thought handshakes were just for greeting, but I still had a lot to learn.

"I've got a case right now that I need help with. My own client is lying to me. He's admitting to a murder." Bill waved his hand. "I'll set something up and explain it then. For now, get with Doris — you'll be a 1099, independent contractor. She'll get all the paperwork and your contact information."

A 1099? I thought to Khimmer, the mind of my Nightarmor.

Unknown, Mistress.

I kept my smile, nodding, and hoped that Doris was the secretary outside. She'd been nice and might actually explain what 1099 meant.

Doris, an older woman, sat straight-backed at a neat desk with three open portfolios and a monitor. Blonde hair lightened with gray, she looked up over her glasses as her phone buzzed the moment I stepped out of Bill's office. She had an easy smile which broadened as she listened.

I paused awkwardly on the carpet, waiting for her to finish.

She ended with a quick, efficient response. "Yes." Hanging up her phone, she spun her chair toward a filing cabinet. "Congratulations, Ahnjii." Papers rustled. "I just need a little information." Without looking back, a thin finger crooked and coaxed me closer to the desk. "I'll need ID."

I dug into my pocket and pulled out my phone. During what my friend Tyler guessed was my 26th birthday, they'd given me a holder for the cell that had slots for my Florida State ID, an emergency credit card of Deanna's, and folded up cash. "I've moved." Three days ago, and now I had a new job. "I have a different address." I placed the ID with my goofy smiling photo on her desk. Tyler had been there, making me laugh.

"No problem, Dear." Doris closed the folios on her desk and placed out forms. "We'll get to that part, but you should get your ID updated." She carefully studied my clothes, from choker to boots. "Do you have a button-down shirt and slacks or skirt? Proper shoes? For court."

I was wearing a black bodysuit and jean shorts. Nightarmor formed a choker, bangles and bracelets on my arms, a thin unadorned belt, and knee-high boots. *Proper shoes?* I leaned over to get a view of hers. *Black slippers of leather.* They wouldn't be very good in a fight.

I can form those, Mistress, thought Khimmer. *Would you like me to try now?*

Khimmer had been more intrusive since we'd arrived on Earth. *No,* I thought to them. Everyone had warned me not to change Nightarmor in public. I could get dissected by some government initials.

I nodded to Doris. "Button-down shirt, slacks or skirt, and proper shoes." Tyler and Deanna would have a blast playing dress up. "For court," I confirmed.

"For court."

Fifteen minutes later I stepped out under the brick archways of the massive building that housed Bill's office. The scent of exhaust hung in the air. Strangely, the weather had been cooler for the past few months. Tomorrow would begin the month of February, and Tyler expected it to get warm again. I smiled at the disgruntled man exiting the doors behind me and pulled out my phone to let Tyler know the good news.

"Hey," Tyler answered. Their car started up in the

background. "How'd it go? Never mind, I know you're hired."

I raised up onto my toes. "I am. This'll be way better than the poke place, but no free eats." I hadn't asked, yet I had smelled fried rice. "I don't think."

"I'm parked down the street." Traffic sounded in the background. "I had wanted it to be a surprise. I planned to take you out for lunch to celebrate, but . . ."

"The Pho place?" I rocked from one foot to the next in excitement. Spicy noodles were the best. I grinned and peered into the street, looking for Tyler's beat-up blue car.

"Sorry, love. John never came home last night, and Deanna's freaking out. I can drop you off at your apartment, but I think I should be home to support Deanna."

I felt a little guilty being disappointed about the missed celebration. "I'll go with you to the house. I can walk to my apartment later." If Deanna's boyfriend John hadn't followed his normal schedule, there was a problem. He wasn't the spontaneous type.

ACKNOWLEDGMENTS

April appears to like Ahnjii. Which is good, since I rely on her so much from developmental to proofing. I can't thank her enough. You can thank her at the least for Tyler's name since I was working with something completely different.

Robyn Huss, my editor, works magic on words, turning some of my most difficult prose into elegant reading. If you've come this far in the book, it is because of her efforts. If you're a writer, I encourage you to look at some of the opportunities she offers - http://www.hussediting.com/

October K Santerelli is an amazing sensitivity read editor. Check out his novels and I highly recommend his services.

I blame being enabled to bring these characters to life on the Fireside Group; Tim, Rosemary, Mark, Vail and Katharine and now Sienna. Dianne and Brett from Apex have been there for me. Arrash and Michele from Jody Lynn Nye's DragonCon workshop keep me on task with the most intricate details and loving support.

I still miss David Farland's tireless mentorship. Please pick up one of his books and enjoy the magic he endowed upon the world. Writers, study his lessons at Apex Writers.

Jody Lynn Nye's workshop will always be my go to suggestion for an in-person critique for any aspiring writers. Her insight is invaluable.

The wonderful cover art is by Rebekah at VividCovers! Consider her for your next design.

Thank you.

www.ingramcontent.com/pod-product-compliance
Lightning Source LLC
Chambersburg PA
CBHW020040310726
48970CB00007B/2345